YA Mitcha
Mitchard, Jacquelyn
Now you see her

$16.89
ocm75087913
1st ed.   09/22/2009

DISCARD

NOW YOU SEE HER

NOW
YOU
SEE
HER

By
JACQUELYN MITCHARD

HarperTempest
An Imprint of HarperCollinsPublishers

This is a work of fiction. It is not intended to recount actual events that may have happened to any living person. Any errors about the thoughts and behaviors of an actor or an emotionally troubled young person are entirely the author's.

HarperTempest is an imprint of HarperCollins Publishers.

Now You See Her

Text copyright © 2007 by Jacquelyn Mitchard

HarperCollins Children's Books, a division of HarperCollins Publishers,
1350 Avenue of the Americas, New York, NY 10019.
www.harperteen.com
Library of Congress Cataloging-in-Publication Data is available.
ISBN-10: 0-06-111683-1 (trade bdg.)—ISBN-13: 978-0-06-111683-4 (trade bdg.)
ISBN-10: 0-06-111684-X (lib. bdg.)—ISBN-13: 978-0-06-111684-1 (lib. bdg.)
Typography by Larissa Lawrynenko
1 2 3 4 5 6 7 8 9 10

First Edition

For the real Alyssa Lyn,
I love nieces to pieces

NOW YOU SEE HER

I

HOPE IS VANISHING.

Does that sound too dramatic?

Okay, fine. It's really just barely dramatic enough. Maybe not even enough.

I don't mean "hope" the way they think. How could I explain it to them? They're beyond stupid. They're clueless and retarded. All of them. I hear my mother and father say, "She doesn't realize the gravity of all this. . . ." and I want to yell, Are you crazy? Are you on crack?

I'm the one it happened to. So I, like, sort of understand the *gravity*. I had the bruises on my wrists for weeks. I wouldn't even go outside to walk to the classroom building from my gorgeous dorm here for months, either. And I still won't go out at night. I don't even like to look out the window when it's dark.

Let's try this again, class. This time with motions!

I was a girl with a gift, who was totally going places, and now I'm the girl no one will ever know except as "that Hope somebody-or-other, the girl who vanished." Well, at least for the time being, until I can straighten everyone's head out. That's not exactly fun and games!

My mother used to say that every news story, even a bad review, was good if they spelled your name right. Good for an actor, that is. (We never said "actress" in our house. That was for people who didn't know any better. Anyone who's serious about acting is an "actor," even if they're a girl.) What my mother meant was that someday I'd be on Broadway or in the movies or have CDs with my name on them bigger than the title of the CD, and then we wouldn't care less what people thought of my performances, because I'd be wonderful and I'd know it!

I don't think she had this in mind!

What's really *grave* is *the effect on me*. They talk about everything that happened right in front of me like I'm not there. They don't see me. When you don't see someone, she disappears. That's why I'm vanishing. And not the way the police and the school said. And definitely not the way the newspapers said.

Let me try to show you how I feel right now. This is my All-About-Me Journal you're seeing. (Sweet Jesus, we all have to do these. I haven't written stuff like "Gee, I like kitties and pizza and birthday parties and the color pink" since the first grade! That's what they actually want us to write! One day's assignment, I swear, was a list of All The Things I Like About Me.) Every time I make an entry, I have to date it. Except I won't date it, because that's what Miss Taylor wants me to do, so I use a mark of my own, just to piss her off. Look back: See that little "I"? At the top of the first page? That "I," it could be a Roman Numeral One. Or it could be a person's self! Your ego, who you are.

Your "I."

That's how big I feel. As big as that little letter. And getting smaller and smaller and smaller.

I'm shrinking outside—and I was already very, very thin—but I'm shrinking inside, too. Down to a little, little mouth with a tiny, squeaky voice that says "Help me." Like Alice in Wonderland, when she drank from the bottle that said, "Drink Me." (Or was it when she ate the cake? I don't remember.) But if I don't find the reverse potion fast, there's going to be nothing left. It's unbelievable.

I'm sure my parents are very concerned. Everyone here at my new school says my parents are very, very concerned.

But if I had to bet, I would bet my mother cried that morning at the school when they told her what happened. Then she would have blotted her mascara with tissue. Not to get carried away. That would be so un-Marian.

When they finally brought me to my parents, that's exactly what she did. I saw it! Two perfect, elegant tears, and then blot, blot, let's not wreck the look! Let's not stain the Kate Spade sweater! There I was—cold and dirty and bruised and dehydrated and scared to death, and my mother just wanted to make sure her "face," as she calls it, was still perfect. My dad at least messed his hair up, and kept muttering to the police things like "That seems impossible." Or, "How could she have done that?" And, "No, that was her mother's sister, not her sister. We only have one other child, a son." Or, "Are you sure?"

And he might have been pulling on his tie and messing up his hair, but he sure was *not* all over me with kisses and relief and joy. I sure wasn't his little princess then, his superstar, his little stick of dynamite—all those things he'd called me when he came running to the stage door, night after night, every time I was in a show for the past eight years! He acted like none of that had ever happened. He didn't pick me up and swing me around and give me a big bouquet of yellow roses (our special flower, though I read somewhere it means betrayal).

They looked at me like the princess who turned into a frog.

It made me think, Really, did they ever really care? About me? The real me? Was there a real me—to them?

Or was it just, ever so casually, "Oh, Hope got the lead in this. . . . Hope won that competition in Los Angeles. . . ." My mom used to find a way to work every conversation around to me being an actor—it was like *she* won the competition or got the role. It was all she could ever talk about, and I can't imagine how she would go on when I wasn't even there to get embarrassed and tell her to shut the hell up or I would walk out of the house. And when I would just do normal kid things, which was not very often (I had to sleep ten hours and in a cucumber mask!), she wouldn't even notice me, except when I was walking out. She'd say, "Don't eat fries, Hopie. Use your skin lotion, Hopie."

I can't blame the kids I used to go to school with for hating my guts when I got paid hundreds or even thousands of dollars for being in a commercial or a play—or even acting in the regional theater group when I couldn't get something that paid. I was better than they were—I don't mean better at acting; I mean, just better, and prettier, and more grown-up. They must have thought I was totally stuck-up because I didn't go out for burgers or stay over or go to the nine o'clock movie. You can't expect regular people to understand. I know that. Kids thought I was nuts that I gave up going to the pool (tanning wrecks your skin) and Disney World (no time) and all that junk for "my art."

But my parents! They made me who I am! You'd think they'd want to at least protect and take care of the girl they gave ten hundred lessons, the girl they took to ten hundred auditions. I remember them sending me up to the studio or agent's office. (They would stand downstairs and smoke. They thought I didn't know.) I can remember them saying afterward they were "just sure" I'd done the best of anyone . . . but did I remember to smile on the word "super"? Was I sure? You'd have thought my parents would at least think of how valuable I was, and how dear to them, and how damned hard I tried for them. For me too, of course. For me too.

But all I had to do was get in trouble once (never mind that I had nothing to do with it!), and they went cold as the ice on the lake.

Maybe all they ever cared about anyway was how things looked. That's it. How things looked to the gourmet group and the Fine Arts Council and the Bellamy Country Club.

Not me.

The Gift.

Yeah, what they cared about was The Gift.

It's like I'm just a coat that was wrapped around The Gift.

I remember it all. When I was twelve and I made, like, half a noise about wanting to be a cheerleader for just one year. And they were, like, "You have a *gift*, Hope. And we've spent years and a great deal of money developing that gift . . . but we want you to be happy, and if you want to give it up, we'll understand. . . ."

Well, I didn't then, not after a complete guilt trip! The next week I was back getting a song ready to try out for some Christmas show at the Civic Center.

And they liked me again.

It was as if The Gift and I were two *people*, two separate people.

Only one of them—Hope—nobody cared about. And nobody does still, I guess!

The Gift always wanted more, and always got what it wanted. The Gift wanted me acting and singing in plays, being in commercials, and someday being in movies. The Gift was my parents' little medal they could take out and wear.

When I was little, it was just fun. When I got a little bigger, it wasn't so much fun.

And then, when I got old enough that I actually could have stopped acting if I wanted to—they couldn't have forced me—I was obsessed with it. And plus, there isn't anything else I could ever do. The world of backstage in a theater, the smell of makeup and dust and chalk, is more real to me than my own bedroom. My parents made sure of that. They dragged me to Broadway shows that were written when *they* were kids. Revivals, they called them. And you practically had to revive me after I saw one, like *Oklahoma!* Because it was so boring. But they said if I wanted to be a big movie star, I had to "pay my dues" on the stage. All really famous actors did. They loved "the stage." For me, until I got used to it, I could never understand how you wouldn't go bonkers saying the same words over and over and over every day. But then, I got to know, like every time a singer sings a song, even if it's their famous song they've done a thousand times, it feels different. And people go crazy over you. There's nothing like people going crazy over you. That's what you want, even more than the money.

My mother would tell me how she and her two sisters, Maggie and Marjorie, went to every Broadway show when it opened and sat in the cheapest seats with their grandmother. How her grandmother taught my mom to play the piano, though my mother can't do it anymore. Even when I was little, before I got addicted to the applause and the attention, my mom was already addicted to it for me. She was going to be an actor when *she* was young, but I picked up that her parents made her get married instead. She got married, like, four months after she met my father. You had to then if you were pregnant. Her sister Marjorie was going to be a dancer. She didn't do it either. She quit. Her other sister had no talent except for a little singing, and she didn't do it long. And she ended up as a biology professor.

See, if you don't care about what my mother cares about, you don't count. Just like her sister (my mother calls her "the frog dissection queen") doesn't count, even though she used to sing. It was Aunt Maggie's choice to quit. Something happened to Aunt Marjorie—maybe she pulled a groin muscle or something. I don't remember. Anyhow, she didn't have to quit. If you have The Gift and quit anyhow, you don't count.

Now I don't count.

Which makes no sense because it wasn't my decision. You know what I expected, after all I'd been through? I really thought I'd get taken care of at home kind of carefully for part of a semester, like someone who'd been sick. Instead, they started driving, and I thought we were going home so I went to sleep in the backseat. Until they turned in to Miss Taylor's I didn't know a thing.

I was so pissed off that I punched my dad and told him what a lying crap he was. I wouldn't get out of the car, so they sent this beautiful but wacko girl, Suzette, who has, like, four zillion tattoos, down to talk to me. Suzette told me I could sit there until I starved to death and I would still have to come in anyway. She said she wanted to sing in a metal band but her parents wanted her to go to Yale, so guess who won? After that, I could tell it was no use.

My parents were going to get their way. At least temporarily. They couldn't wait to get me stuck away here. All nice and out of sight. Nothing to embarrass the Romanos once the big hoopla died down in the newspapers. But after that, my parents didn't come to see me for a month! And I was only allowed to call them once because I was supposed to get used to my new environment and "trust" it. I'm so sure.

I think they're embarrassed. They've done so much bragging about me to their friends—the guys with their red martini noses and the women with their lips so stuffed with collagen they look like a bass or a goldfish. Now those "friends" have something juicy to gossip about. It's probably get-even time for them. They can talk about me, but that's because their own kids have no talent. They practically have no lives. Their fat daughters are good in *math*! Or *history*! That's so fine. Except math and history don't make you famous. Name one person who's famous for math.

Okay, Einstein.

The kids were always jealous of me, but the parents were worse. It must have been awful for them to have kids who were so dull and ordinary. The girls whose feet got so big they would never make it past city in gymnastics, even if they took lessons until they were forty, and the boys all covered with zits and sitting with their shoulders humped over in their DeathZone T-shirts and their ear buds in, bobbing up and down.

But the thing is, *they're* home. They'll probably all turn out normal. *Normal.* Like lawyers and teachers.

But who wants to be normal? I used to think, Hello! No one? But now I don't know. I guess it would be better, considering this mess. I used to feel sorry for the Neeland kids and Abby, my so-called friend from the theater group, but they don't have to write stupid journals and do twice the homework of an ordinary high school like I do because this is an *exclusive* prep school. I'm the one who was so special. Their parents wouldn't just sweep them under the rug when something happened to them. My parents did. They basically swept me under the rug. I wonder if rape victims feel this way.

Even now, my parents have only come to visit two times. For two hours. They say it's the rules. But I think it's that my mother's convinced I'm nuts or something. Stuff does happen around here that doesn't sound normal. But hello! Stuff happened back in Bellamy that would have freaked them out, and in Starwood, too! I can remember sitting in the back of the bus in, like, eighth grade in Bellamy—which is supposed to be as rich as Palm Springs or someplace—and hearing girls say, "I get high and I get drunk and then I do it! I don't care who with! As long as he's cute!" What would my parents have thought of perfect Starwood if they knew about the deserted cabin? And don't think my brother, Carter, doesn't know about that stuff, just like I did! Now when my dad talks, I bet it's all about Carter, Carter, Carter, who they just sort of let grow up and play soccer before. They can't talk about me anymore. They had to go to the reserve kid.

I know because when my dad does bother to come, he's like, "Carter's turning out really good. Carter's on the honor roll. Carter's getting really tall." It's like Carter grew out of the ground like a magic mushroom after the kidnapping.

Before, they didn't even notice they had two kids.

Well, they're going to notice me again.

First of all, I'm practically starving away to nothing because I won't eat the garbage Miss Taylor calls food.

I heard my father say they were hitting him up for twenty big ones a year for tuition. You'd think for that much, they could afford better than baked beans and iceberg lettuce! *Canned* beans? Iceberg lettuce? I never had those things in my entire life. And sauerkraut? Who eats sauerkraut? Oh God, I ran into the hall bathroom and yakked the first time I even smelled it. And they make it, like, twice a month because it's cheap. Even the teachers are cheap because they can only get jobs at places like Miss Taylor's. Everyone knows private school teachers suck.

My parents aren't going to get away with it, and Logan isn't going to get away with it.

It's too much.

Oh shit. I should be done with this by now.

I wrote and wrote and wrote, and I still have to write five more pages. In my *own* handwriting. It's more "authentic" than the computer. You have to write *more* the first few months to "get your feelings down on paper." Okay.

Retards.

Assholes.

Second verse, same as the first!

Think of it this way: say that one day you were this girl who was, well, it.

It.

I'm not bragging.

I was. I was the person that other people wanted to be like. Like a trendsetter, a person who had this style of her own, where there were only preps and Goths, basically. Not just at home, but at Starwood, too. It was natural for people to copy whatever I wore. I was so much more adult. I knew how to wear clothes. Real clothes, not kid clothes. I wore tight capri pants under dresses with straps and other people did too. I could wear a scarf and not look like someone's mother. (You don't just throw it on; you have to know how to tie it.) I wore ballet shoes for real shoes. Other girls started doing it too. When I did my hair up in these tiny little rows of colored pins, other girls did too. When I got gigantic shades, other girls got their parents to send them the same kind, and layered their short skirts over long skirts, even when it just made them look like fat asses. They even pronounced words how I pronounced words. It was almost annoying.

That's what it's like to be it.

And then there was this big total misunderstanding that I was just led into! You'd think, with it being someone like me, they would believe in me a little. *No!* They blame me. Not Logan. He's fine and dandy. He's a real *actor*, even in real life! He lies and they believe him. I'm the one thrown out of Starwood. My school doesn't stick up for me. My parents don't stick up for me. My so-called boyfriend acts like we never even met.

And I end up here.

Some of the girls, they really need to be here. It's the best they can do. But if you were . . . something, not just something—if you were it, then it's hard to come down to this. I had more to lose, you know? I'm not being conceited. It's just the truth.

Wouldn't you be pissed off? Or more? Like, desperate?

Wouldn't you just cry and cry and cry? I do! Me! I cry

like one of the idiot girls I used to go to school with in Bellamy. They cried over their retarded boyfriends or that their best friends didn't invite them to a sleepover or that they got *grounded* and couldn't go to the *big game*! Stuff that never even affected me.

I never cried.

Well, not never.

I used to cry from anger when I got to the last round of callbacks only to lose out to some Barbie doll. Callbacks are when they invite you back on another night to audition again for a show, after they weed out all the zero-talent blobs and fatsos. I cried over stuff like that, even when my mother said, "They were just look-ing for a particular type, honey. . . ." I cried just recently when my dog, Hero, died without ever getting to see me again.

I cried over Logan.

And now I walk around like a zero among negative numbers. Wearing my Miss Taylor's uniform, my black-watch plaid skirt and red blazer. Ohmigod. I look like the American Girl doll I had when I was little, the one they would never let me play with. Like this outfit was designed by a blind nun! I swear. *Loafers* with a little hole for a penny! No jewelry, not even little diamond studs. My ear holes are going to grow together. I take *Latin*! I have to sing in a choir in chapel! And when I start to really sing, they say, "Now remember, this is unison singing. No stars here—we're all stars!" We all have to walk together to meals and sit next to a different girl every time. I have to spend one hour every night minimum writing in this stupid-ass journal. I'm learning to play lacrosse and *soccer*! Please! Is it any wonder that crying is, like, all I do? I am crying my head off, and no one cares.

Except this one girl who lives on my hall, Em.

That's what I should write about.

Em. She is so sweet. Like, a really good person. Though she probably does belong in a very strict school like this. She has big issues. I mean . . . big!

I saw her the first day. She was shy. Just sort of slipping around the corners in the hall. But she reminded me of someone. She had this long curly black hair, and she would have been pretty if she hadn't been so fat. She was graceful. I found out later that was because she'd been a ballerina. We got to be friends, like, right away. She still hardly ever says anything. But I can tell that she understands. This one day, she smiled when she walked past. She has this beautiful, sad smile. So I wrote a note to her. I slipped it under her door. Now, I write things to her all the time, and when she sees me, she smiles. When I talk to her, instead of looking straight at me, she's smart enough to act like she's looking out in the distance. I know she's listening, though. Sometimes, when she's heard me through the wall at night, crying, she has tears in her own eyes the next morning at breakfast, and makes the okay sign at me.

Like it could ever be okay.

I'm crying and crying all the time, except I never get to float or drown like Alice in Wonderland almost did, in a river of her own tears. A river of her own tears.

I told Em about that. She thought it was beautiful. It was her favorite book when she was little too. She wanted to go to another world too, away from this boring, ugly one, with people with blackheads on their nose and Cheetos on their breath. When I was little, my mother would tie my hair back with these sparkly velvet bands, and my father would say I was his Alice in Wonderland.

I told Em about Logan. About Logan and his big Plan. For ruining my life. And how he won't answer his phone: "Logan here. Speak." How he's at Starwood, having a ball. Probably literally. Probably with Alyssa Lyn Davore. Getting a scholarship to Carnegie Mellon. Never thinking of me. Glad he's out of it.

And I'm here.

Em. She's a great listener, and she's funny and smart the two days a month when she's only mildly chemically imbalanced. I can tell by the notes she sends back to me.

Sometimes they're just little cartoon drawings. Sometimes they say, like, "Just be sure not to be yourself!" When she's out on one of her whippy trips, you could be talking to your basic floor lamp. She doesn't even react. But she's not like that all the time.

If it wasn't for Em, I'd be gone now. Gone. As in dead. Like the real Juliet, not the girl I was playing at Starwood.

You know *Romeo and Juliet*? I mean, the Shakespeare play, not the movie? God, you have to. Everybody is forced to read it in high school. Well, I was the star. I was Juliet. In the play, Juliet got married on Sunday and she was dead by Thursday. She killed herself. She stabbed herself with a dagger! That's why it's so famous, such a famous tragedy. She was only fourteen, younger than me! Imagine being Juliet, and then a few weeks later being told you could never act again, when it was your life, your whole life. All because of a stupid freaking trick by a stupid guy.

I'm so sure. I'm so sure that's what I'll do. Never act again.

Maybe become a nice accountant. Or a dentist!

By now, if it wasn't for the fact that Em sort of needs me as a role model for surviving prep school, I'd probably have taken a hundred Tylenol PM. She needs me, and also, I think taking Tylenol like that damages your liver if you don't die. I read that some people in England took some kind of painkiller and they woke up and their livers were destroyed and they were going to die and they had to sit there for a couple of days? Just waiting to die?

They probably didn't even really want to die in the first place, and probably didn't take enough on purpose. How retarded can you get? If I did it, I would do it right, like Juliet. So they couldn't save me. I'd do it beautifully. Falling down on my bed in the moonlight. Some nights, on top of my comforter in my crummy bunk, I imagine I'm lying in my casket, in Juliet's wedding costume, with the little velvet cap on my hair. I'd leave a note to make sure that my parents would buy it from Starwood. That would be the least they could do. And there would be music. Like Pachelbel's "Canon." I know, it's a cliché, but everyone knows it and it makes people get all weepy. Or "Clair de Lune." Because I'm so young and I'll never look at the moon again. Or what is it? "Pavane for a Dead Princess"? My parents made me listen to all that classical crap, along with show tunes, when I took piano lessons. I got imprinted on it like a little duck, and now it's always the soundtrack when I imagine my life as a movie. I don't even know the songs kids my age know.

Yes. It would be so sad.

Classical and sad. Classy and sad!

My parents also used to read me poems and make me

memorize them to train my memory. It worked. I can memorize whole pages of lines in a few hours. Like there was this one, "Brightness falls from the air . . . queens have died, young and fair. . . ." I have no idea who wrote that. But my mom read it to me when I was little. I just saw it again in a magazine story about Princess Diana dying all those years ago. And I thought how it would be perfect for someone to read for my eulogy. Just one little piece of poetry. Maybe one of the kids from when I was in Saint Barnard's Players in eighth grade. Like Abby would want to do it. Abby totally worshipped me. And she would be falling apart, sobbing while she was reading it. I can see it. I can hear her.

How would Logan feel then? Totally like shit. Totally like the turd he is. Standing there looking at the body of the girl he said he loved.

That would be worth it.

But he's so into himself. I don't even know anymore if Logan has feelings, or if he just pretends he has them to impress people. He'd probably pretend he was so totally worn down by sadness. *I cared so much. I did everything I could.* . . . I can hear him saying it. What a total liar. I'm so not the one in denial! He'd probably feel like he deserved all this pity and compassion and junk when he wasn't even dead! Girls would probably be falling all over to comfort him. They'd be dressed up and have push-up bras on and be smelling of perfume. I'd be lying there like this tiny little queen, but he'd be standing there with his head on somebody else's shoulder.

It would be a big risk another way, too.

Like, would he even bother to come? Would his parents let him? Maybe they'd think it was too traumatic for poor, poor Logan. After all *he's* been through. What if he couldn't even say a final good-bye to me in my tomb? I'd be dead forever, and even if the funeral was really good, he might not go. I wouldn't know if he was there or not. Maybe I wouldn't even be getting back at him!

You know your life is crap when it's not even worth killing yourself.

I'm going to get back at him. Maybe just by being better than him.

That's why I follow the rules.

Like the "jam sessions." That's what she calls them. The Miss Taylor we never see. Our wonderful leader. She sends some teacher or teacher-in-training every week to be the "moderator." You don't have to attend but it's "encouraged." Ohmigod. Wednesday nights in our "pajamas." Our dorm group meetings. I wear my nice flannel pants and long T-shirts. Suzette comes practically naked, in a thong with a see-through top. In front of girls, so the reason would be . . . what? Em wears big men's striped pj's if she's okay. If she's not, she wears whatever she's been wearing all week—like *all* week, including the same underwear, day and night. It's so meaningless. You know what it's like when adults pretend to listen and you can see them thinking about other crap? You can *see* them thinking, Oh, I should get my highlights touched up. Or, Oh, I forgot to make an appointment for Devon's cavity. And all the while they're nodding and saying, "I can see why you feel that way," and acting like you can't tell that their laptop means more to them than you do.

A healthy mind in a healthy body for the well-rounded young woman. That's the Taylor motto. That's what all that running up and down in the freezing cold chasing a ball with a stick on wet grass is for!

Half the teachers are *really* well-rounded. They didn't used to be actors, or aren't still actor wannabes, just barely over the hill, the way the Starwood teachers are. Like, one has a waist the size of one of my mother's exercise balls.

Em's waist is too, though.

Em looks like the Queen of Hearts after she ate the tarts.

I mean this in a totally nice way.

Once I passed her door and it was open. I saw her literally unloading her secret stash of Snickers, which she had stuffed in everything from her purse to her gym shorts. (Yeah, we have to wear gym uniforms, like rejects from parochial schools.) Not that Em isn't totally sweet. But how could you eat something you had kept hidden all day inside your clothes? It skeves me out just to think about it. I took a good look at her. Em is tall, like five eleven, like my mother, but she is massive. I thought that day (I didn't know her very well yet) that if I didn't lock my door, she'd eat *me* in my sleep. She held out one of the candy bars to me. I was like, uh, no thanks, but thanks. I thought, Where does she get them? They don't have a bookstore with T-shirts and candy and star stickers and lattes and stuff like they did at Starwood. I just waved and crept away from her door. I pretended I didn't notice the food on the bed. She looked so ashamed.

Taylor should probably be helping her with her obsession with food, but all I've seen our "helpers" do is reduce Em to tears instead of a size six. She should probably be at a school that concentrates on, you know, fat. She should talk about why she can't get through a day without six candy bars at seven hundred calories apiece. I mean, fat ballerinas have limited appeal? She ate herself right out of the Concord Academy. She never used to be fat, she tells me in her notes. Her "freshman fifteen" turned into a freshman forty.

I just have to hold on. I have to make sure they don't get to me.

So, even though I don't have obsessions, I make them up for our "jam sessions," which I don't even know why we have because no one is really mental.

Even Suzette. Suzette just has to talk about her obsession with her brother dying in a car accident while she was driving or something and why it makes her want to fail in school and have sex constantly. Personally, I think Suzette is just a little over the top. Anyone would feel the way she does. She liked her brother, like, a lot. They were close, even though he was only eight or something. Suzette probably doesn't need to be at a school as military as Taylor's.

There are other girls who have academic problems and junk—like having flunked out of three other schools, including public, for smoking, drinking Scotch and milk, or cutting class for four weeks straight. One even slapped her cheerleading supervisor.

See the difference? Watch carefully now! They actually *did* something, even Suzette and poor Em. Although I will say none of the stories are as interesting as what happened to me. None of them were on the news. Well, maybe Suzette's brother was, but only in the local paper, because they probably felt sorry for the family.

I have to come up with something to be obsessed with, because I'm supposed to, so I say my mother came from a family where her father beat her mother, and her sisters were totally screwed up, and one killed herself with a dagger. I say that I'm afraid of being buried alive. Whoever the teacher or teacher's aide is that night gets all excited. They probably think they're psychologists.

Mostly, when I'm not having a sharing moment (vomit!), I just listen to them. Or if I can't stand it, I pretend to. I sit and stare out the leaded-glass windows and try to remember old monologues, so I don't totally lose my brain. If I say something, no one cares. Everyone here is either spaced-out or thinks they're all that because their parents are so rich or whatever.

I end up turning out my cheap light every night when I'm done with my "journaling" and scream in the night, biting my comforter, without making one sound: Logan, pick up your phone just once! Just so I can hang up on you, even! But then I wake up in the morning alive, looking out another leaded-glass window across the room (what did this place used to be, a cathedral? And how the hell old is it?) to eat scrambled eggs that are like the rubber ones that came with my toy frying pan I had when I was five. It made sizzling noises so you could pretend you were really cooking.

How can this all have happened so fast?

Two months ago. Nine weeks ago. I was having final fittings for my gowns. I had to have a whole other set of costumes from Alyssa because she was about twenty pounds heavier than I was. Like, do you know what it means for a sophomore, a fifteen-year-old, to be cast with *seniors*? And not just any seniors—one of them had been in a movie, and one had been off-Broadway. And I was totally holding my own, totally living in those beautiful words, those gauzy paintings of castles behind us. I had everything down to the tiniest movement of one of my hands. At, like, one of the best arts prep schools on Earth. I could feel the understanding begin deep down inside me, coming from the source of all the grief you have from your genes or whatever: "O, swear not by the moon, the inconstant moon, that monthly changes in her circled orb, lest that thy love prove likewise variable." I knew it. I loved it. I was living it, onstage and off. Brooks Emerson, the guy who starred in that play based on the Cervantes story on Broadway, was totally in tears almost, because I was so great.

He was.

I would have gotten into Juilliard.

That's what Logan said. Logan Rose, my Romeo. Who screwed it all up. Screwed my life. Screwed me.

Now I'm in the Wildflowers dorm with Suzette the tattooed lady and Em the hippo ballet dancer—the crash-and-stash rejects from arts high school. At least we're not in Buttercups, with the gaga freshmen and the technology weenies eating their Ritalin.

I so don't need this kind of idiot place.

I need it like Ophelia needed swimming lessons.

Ophelia? She was Hamlet's girlfriend? And he totally rejected her, even though she would never love anyone else, so she drowned herself. The average teenage kid probably thinks of Shakespeare as something you get SparkNotes for, so you can write a boring paper on it. They probably don't even know what it really means. But then, most kids watch those stupid shows on music channels where the girls are so dumb they, like, cry when a guy asks them to *prom*. And kids think those girls are really super-cool.

All I need is someone to listen to me and believe I'm telling the truth. And then all of this can end and I can go back to the way I was. Get out of here. Get started again. Back to who I was.

Before Logan.

Before the kidnapping.

II

I BET THEY TALKED a lot about hope those first few days. Not Hope, as in my name. Hope as in the hope of finding me. When we were driving to Miss Taylor's, my father sort of sketched in what the main police officer and the security chief told them . Probably to lull me into thinking that nothing was wrong. He said that the first day, he felt pretty good because the police said they had never failed to find a missing person. Starwood is a hundred acres, and they said that sounded really big, but basically most of it was buildings and fields. There were only a couple of patches of woods, and the whole thing was fenced off. The national forest land didn't start until the other side of that fence. Later my parents told me that the first day, the police chief and the security officer said there was "every hope" I would be found alive and well.

Today's entry.

See the two little Roman numerals on the first page? Like little stick figures side by side?

Those could be my parents, very tall and elegantly thin (I'm little, like my father's sister). Stiff from fear and, um, yes, embarrassment, they stand side by side, probably for the first time since their wedding day. I can totally picture them. Standing in the dean's office at Starwood Academy of the Performing Arts, with five or six detectives and the dumbest canine "officer" on Earth. (I saw the dog later. That dog wouldn't have been able to find barbecue beef in a deli.) I wasn't there in the room with my parents, obviously. But they would have looked nice. They would have been thinking about themselves, and about how it would look to the neighbors if I was found raped and strangled or something: *The Romano girl? The beautiful one who was an actress? Who changed her name? Right, Mark and Marian's daughter! Well, that's what you get.* . . . Like, being raped and strangled would have been *my* fault. What happened to me was almost as bad.

Twelve hours later, after there was a search that even all these store owners and resort owners and farmers and fishermen joined in, it wasn't so hopeful, and my parents would have looked a little haggard, but still well groomed.

It was November.

In Michigan it's already cold in November. Pure, white Christmas cold, sometimes even by Halloween.

My mother would have been wearing . . . okay, I can do this without even half thinking about it: She would have had on olive slacks with a crease, and a sweater with a rust-colored scarf and earrings to match, because color, she always used to say, must "travel up." She taught me that when other girls were learning the alphabet. It was why I could make normal clothes look like date clothes. She would have dressed carefully. Just because I was missing in Michigan in the winter didn't mean my mother had to look anything but complete Bellamy Country Club.

The first thing that happened when they got to Starwood from the bed and breakfast where they were staying, my father said, was that the dorm advisor told them her story.

She was always a bitch—an opera major who went to graduate school two days a week at Northern Michigan University. Always telling me what I was doing wrong. "We have to make sure our beds are made, Hope," and "We don't go outside at night without an escort, Hope." She came in bawling. She'd already been screaming and crying and showing off for a newspaper reporter earlier that day. She told my parents and the police about how hard it was to find one of her girls missing, and how terrified she was when she saw the videotape, which, though I didn't see it, I know was completely faked. It had to be, or she would have seen me let Logan in, and she kept saying I was alone. Why? I think Logan's parents paid Starwood to protect him. That was the only way it could have happened.

The dean was there too. Knowing her, and that she also was a total and extreme bitch, she was mostly there to comfort my dorm advisor and make sure the school didn't look bad in any of this. My father said the dean told them that I'd probably hitchhiked to Black Sparrow Lake and got myself a hotel room to think things over after the breakup with Logan. She said in a newspaper story I read later that "girls like me" tended to be "very dramatic and high-strung" when it came to failed relationships. She would have seen the stupid faked videotape and thought I went out by myself! Okay, they caught me once for going out at night for a jog. Once! Big deal!

How does jogging at night when it's hot during the day mean you're dramatic and high-strung? I always did my run at night at home! God, I wish I would have been there!

Breakup?

Right.

Like there was even any "breakup" that I knew about!

I would have told them right then what really happened.

And like I so would have hitchhiked. Nobody hitch-hikes, even in a hick place like Black Sparrow Lake. Not unless you're on drugs! You're asking to be raped! I so wanted to be picked up and strangled next to a tree like the poor girl in Central Park. That happened right across from where we lived when I was a baby.

By the second day, it was the biggest manhunt they ever had in the north woods.

Ever.

It was all over the news as far away as California. It was on the radio. There were bulletins with that electronic tone they make before they tell you there's a tornado warning on the radio. I looked up some of the articles in the library and copied them on the machine. It was on TV, too. I know my parents were interviewed. There were helicopters and police all the way from Detroit. There were federal agents.

It was the biggest thing that had happened in history, well, in *Michigan* history, except the time when a college girl was murdered by her ex-boyfriend. That was all the way in Ann Arbor and, like, a year before. It was even bigger than when that little boy walked away from the family's campsite with his dog the summer before. Now, the little boy was deep in the woods, not on a campus that was only a hundred acres. It was a complete miracle they found him. He was almost dead. It should have been much easier to find me. I would have been totally visible, in the rut beside the jogging path. I would have been smell-able to that stupid cop-dog or search dog or whatever he was. The second dog was a lot smarter, apparently, though I never got a real look at that one. That's where I got thrown, into the rut; but I scooched myself up. I couldn't move, but I could see the idiots go clomping by, like, four times. I was almost dead, too. From shock and fear, if not actual injuries. Yes, they released me from the hospital after only a few hours, but that was what I wanted. I was suffering from exposure and dehydration, and I would have gotten frostbite if it had gotten any colder, because the third night it went down to ten degrees. Ten degrees and Logan never came to check on me! He totally chickened out, and I read how he said he would do anything to help search for me because I was a "really special person."

Can you believe such crap?

By the time they found me, there were like sixty or a hundred reporters camped out at the school in vans with satellites on top. All these beautiful reporters and handsome anchors were all trying to interview me—some I even recognized—when I was carried by on the stretcher. They were all calling me "honey" and "Hopie" and saying I was "so brave." I looked like shit, and that was really awful. I couldn't even brush my hair before they took pictures of me. I had burrs in my hair. And my parents wouldn't let me talk to anyone. I'm sure they really were sad at that point. They made like a ring around me with some teachers and the dean and the paramedics.

I would have told them the truth right then! With the reporters and all! After all, besides my brother, Carter, I'm their only child. And Carter wasn't exactly on their agenda until I tanked out.

I was the family hope, which isn't a pun.

"You'll be famous one day," my mother said. "People all over the country will know your name."

Well, Mom, you were right.

Now where are you?

III

S EE THOSE THREE little numerals up there?
Think of them as us: Mom and Dad and me, at
the Starwood auditions.

Me in the middle.

I was exactly fourteen and a half. I was freaking out.

Back in Bellamy, I had been sort of a star.

It started with community theater, but then, when I
was eleven, I went to an open call for this old-time musical about a little orphan girl named Annie at the Bellamy
Lakeshore Dinner Theater. An open call is just exactly
what it sounds like. It's a tryout for a show that anyone
can come to, but most of the people who come . . . it's
embarrassing. Like, you can hardly hear them when they
sing, or they forget the words to their monologues and
have to go ask their mothers, and you can see the director trying hard not to shrink down in his chair, and then

he says, "Very nice, thank you," and the person, like, turns red as a mosquito bite and runs out of the room. You can tell the people you have to worry about right away, too, because either they just go marching up to the person playing the piano and tell them the key to play their song in, or you've seen them before, or they've spent the whole waiting time kind of goofing off with their friends or their parents.

I hated seeing people like that, because it totally meant that my chances were less. Anyhow, this Bellamy Lakeshore Dinner Theater was small but respected. It was Equity. I would get paid, like, union scale, five hundred a day for three performances a week for three weeks. I think it was that much, or even more. And I would get my union card. That means you're a member of the actors' union, which is a professional group that protects actors from people who would work them to death. You get to have dinner breaks and stuff if it's an Equity production.

I got called back, but all the other girls were older and real dancers. One had naturally curly red hair and freckles, and I thought, Why am I doing this? (I have straight, dark brown hair and olive skin, because my dad is Italian.) Annie was supposed to be a cute little girl with curly red hair. My mother had rented the movie and we watched it. There was no way. They would want me to be one of the skinny orphan girls.

They made us sing the song about Annie thinking that maybe her mother cooks and sews and has made her a closet of clothes, and I got this sob in my voice, without losing control of my breath. I started thinking, What if my own mother didn't exist? I realized I might miss her. I was trying to think if she'd ever made me a Halloween costume or if we had ever done an art project together. I couldn't remember that we ever had. She ran lines with me. She read poems to me and made me repeat them. She read her novels in the same room with me while I practiced piano. But not the other stuff. I got really sentimental about missing this idea of my own mother, a mother I'd never had.

That afternoon, not even four hours later, the director called me and said that I got the part. The girl who really should have been Annie was my understudy. She was fourteen! I almost died. My mother started to cry, one of the only times I ever saw her cry real tears. Usually she faked crying if my father upset her in some way, and she always cried when I sang. But this time she really cried and said, "She's really going to make it. She's really going to go all the way."

I thought she was overdoing it. But she overdoes everything. And it was practically off-Broadway in the Midwest, after all.

My dad could tell I was scared. He was never quite so involved in the acting as my mother, but he knew why I was scared. My dad had perfect pitch. He could really sing. With a couple of martinis in him, he'd quickly remember he'd been a Whiffenpoof, which is the glee club at Yale. He turned out to be a lawyer because his father said acting was a sissy thing, but he had big ambitions for his baby, even though he didn't brag about me like my mom did. "You won't give up like I did," he used to tell me when he was drunk. "You won't end up staring at motions and briefs all day." I had a great voice, too, when I was little. Great for a little kid, that is. Not like the girl in the movie, and not like Judy Garland in *The Wizard of Oz*, though I think she was grown-up and just pretending to be a kid. I had a nice little vibrato and a high C above middle C. And I could belt, which means your voice sounds a whole lot bigger than it is. But by the time I was eleven, I wasn't adding on more high notes like real singers do. My coach taught me lots of tricks to "act" the song, so you wouldn't notice I couldn't quite hit the highs the way I did before. I still had to work harder than other people who matured vocally better than I did. I practiced until the director warned me about overdoing it and hurting my vocal cords. I jogged to increase my lung capacity. I even talked this girl Casey into giving me her asthma inhaler and saying she'd lost it. They make your lungs hold more air. I ended up playing my A game for that show. I pulled it off.

We did the show in the Bountiful Mills Theater, an old cannery made over into a theater with a big stage and lots of fancy tables with candles, named after the cereal company that had its headquarters in Trentville, right outside Bellamy. (My father said that they made the town hole into the town hall.) It was this big fancy theater with stained-glass windows and did look a little out of place across the street from the trailer park where most of the people at the cereal factory lived. Those people didn't go to the theater, but people from Bellamy did, to see the Houston Ballet or the Cleveland Symphony. (My father said that the people who lived in Trentville went to Bellamy—but to fish for channel catfish off the highway bridge.) My mother bought fifty-two tickets, one for practically everyone she knew. Other families who had girls in the show got mad at her for buying up so many seats. People's grandparents couldn't come to opening night because there weren't enough seats. But those people were one of the five hundred little girls in the orphanage, not Annie. Anyway, to make up for it, like an apology, my mother had to make a big donation to the theater company. My mother was totally being selfish, but other mothers' daughters were totally losers, too. I mean, in the chorus, yelling "It's the Hard-Knock Life."

It couldn't have felt the same way for them that it did for me.

I lie in bed and I think of it now. My first big role.

If you are an actor, there's nothing like the first time. The first time you really get that this is what your life is about. The whole world is looking at you. People are *paying* to look at you. You can make them feel anything you want them to feel. I got out onstage, and I felt this strange tingly feeling start in my palms and spread up to my brain. I exploded. I literally exploded. When Annie sang about the mother who's made her a closet of clothes, searching for her baby, I could hear people in the audience sniffling and coughing. Because of me! And I thought, I could do this forever. Not just every night, but forever, without stopping to eat or sleep, until I dropped down dead.

I got my first big write-up in the newspaper.

It wasn't the *Bellamy Herald*, either; it was the *Chicago Tribune*. My mother had a shadowbox made, with the program and a ticket and photos.

And of course, she thought the next step would be a big movie or the stage in New York.

First, she changed my name.

She changed my name! She said Bernadette Romano sounded like the eleventh child in a Catholic family of twelve. So I became Hope Shay. Shay was my mother's maiden name. Hope was my middle name.

She had new composite pictures of me—in jeans, in a man's shirt over a leotard, in my *Annie* costume, and one smoochy glamour-face shot that made me look about twenty. It was weird seeing HOPE SHAY in big bold letters across the top, over a list of what I could do (swim, ride a horse, tennis, ballet—sort of a lie—English accent) and all the stuff I'd acted in. It was also weird, coming back to school after Christmas break and being called "Hope" (or "Dope" or "Mope" after I did this insurance commercial that was on TV all the time, where I had to walk across a room and throw a pom-pom into the air while somebody talked about who would pay for me to go to college if my father died). I could have just gone on with my previous name at school, but my mom said, "Get used to it; it's your legal name now." So I did.

And that summer I became, like, the audition queen. My brother went to stay with my grandma Jeanie in Minnesota while I went city to city to city with my parents. They said I should think of it "like a vacation." I tried out for commercials. I tried out for modeling. But I wasn't thin enough. I tried out for a chorus part in a revival of *Oliver!* on Broadway. I got a callback for that. But by the time I did, I had grown an inch taller, and you had to be five feet tall max—which made me mad because I never got any taller! I went to Best Talent, a contest in California where they bring in, like, two thousand kids from all fifty states. I was one of eight kids who won a first-place award, and a trophy, in acting and a third place in singing. But even I could tell that my third was about a million miles from the first in my age group. I got lots of cards from agents. They all said I should be trying out for sitcoms right away. I was starting to think musical theater wasn't for me. So was my mother. And she was getting frantic.

One night, we were in Milwaukee or someplace, my mom said, "Mark, we have to rent an apartment in L.A. so I can take her out there for pilot season."

Pilot season is when they cast and shoot the shows that are going to be pilots the next year. Sitcoms, or even shows like *Law & Order*, whenever they start a new one. I actually know a kid who plays one of the sons of the main detective on *Law & Order: Street Gang Unit*.

My dad said no. He put his foot down. I couldn't believe it. He actually told my mother I wasn't going to Los Angeles. If my mom wanted me to go to a good arts prep school, that was one thing. But that would be it. They had the biggest fight I've ever seen two people have that wasn't on TV. My mom threw the room service menu at his head. My dad kicked over a chair. He said my mom had pushed me enough, and she wasn't going to hustle my ass for TV shows. He said it just like that. And my mom screamed back at him, "Out there, when you're twenty, you're over the hill! Look at Jodie. . . ."

"Yeah, look at your sister!" my dad yelled right back. Look what happened to her because she was pushed and pushed and pushed. No, if she's going to do this, it's going to be a regular girl's life. A girl with a nice, normal family. And this is just going to be a part of it. That's it, Marian."

"A regular, nice, normal family. Like ours?"

"What's wrong with ours?"

"What's right with it?" she bellowed. "It's boring and small and stupid! All your friends are stupid and small-time! They are so Illinois! My daughter should be in New York at least!"

"That really worked for Marjorie, didn't it?" my dad yelled.

My dad got his way, though. By the time we got home, I was back in regular school, and my dad wouldn't even let me apply to Starwood Academy until I was finished with ninth grade.

But when I did, it was like Best Talent all over again. Nobody knew me and nobody treated me special or hugged me and let me go first when I showed up for an audition. I was just a number. I didn't like it at all. It was creepy, like those auditions where all the other kids seemed to know each other.

There were five of me.

There were *ten* of me.

Twenty.

Hello!

I had been the only one of me in Bellamy, Illinois.

Now I saw all these girls walking around in leg warmers and dance pants pulled down below their belly buttons who could stand with one leg straight up against a pillar in the hall. I'd had, like, two years of ballet when I was little, and no way could I do that. There were kids who had a high D above C, some even more notes than that.

Who *were* these kids?

I went out and sat in the car. My father came stomping out after me and practically ripped the door off its hinges. He was so red in the face he looked like he was going to have a heart attack. He said, "Bernadette." I wouldn't even look at him.

"It's Hope in this setting," I said. I held out my hand, as if I was going to shake hands with him, and he slapped it down. I couldn't believe it. My father!

He said, "Get in there and don't be an ass. You may be Hope Whatever Miss Pain-in-the-Butt on the stage, but you're Bernadette Romano to me. Named after my

sister." And before I could open my mouth to say anything, he pulled me out of the car. "I know what you're
thinking, and I know why," he said. "Anybody would be
intimidated by those kids. But you don't get to give up
before you start."

"I get to do what I want. It's my life," I told him,
pushing him away.

"Not yet," he said. "When it's your life, I'll let you
know."

This was about as much attention as my father had
ever paid to me when he was sober. And he knew what
he was talking about. So, when my turn came, and I sang
"Summertime," which is from this old musical about a
man who had no legs who loved some kind of prostitute
lady, and all of them were African American. And I
sounded really sad, because I was. I didn't have to act it.
My mother had said that was supposed to be a very sad
song. Even though the words said the daddy was rich and
the mom was beautiful, that really wasn't true—the lady
singing it was just trying to be sweet to her little kid
because the father might have died when he was out at
sea, fishing. It freaked me out totally when I saw that
two of the nine judges were black, and I thought they
would hate me for singing that song, but the lady smiled
and nodded. And then, because my dad had yelled at me,
I was very emotional. Next I did the scene from *Our*

Town, which we all had to read when I was back in ninth grade in Bellamy, where Emily's already dead and she comes back and she's begging her mother to really look at her. And I had to think about something, although you're not supposed to think about anything in real life because that takes away from your character, so I thought about all the times I would beg my dad to look at me when I was really, really little and I had dressed up my doll to look exactly like me and how he was always too busy with his stack of motions and briefs and told me to go away. I thought about the little Bernadette I was and how she would walk away so lonely and ashamed, and so when I asked the stage manager to take me back to my grave, the judges all sat up straighter when I sort of cried out something like, "Mama, let's look at one another, really look, while there's still time!"

I felt that same tingly feeling I felt when I was in *Annie*.

The judges all made notes, but nobody applauded. I couldn't see if anyone else had gotten applause because all the auditions were individual and closed. But some of the girls came out all bubbly and hugged their parents. I didn't.

On the drive home, nobody said anything much.

My mother said, "Well, there's always next year."

My father said, "She can wait until college."

When we got my acceptance letter, you'd have thought I got a starring role in a movie made by Steven Spielberg or somebody.

My mom got all new clothes for me. She got a personal shopper from Neiman Marcus to help us. I didn't care because I liked the clothes, even though I would only be able to wear them on weekends because you had to wear uniforms at Starwood. She got me a new laptop and gave Carter my old one. Carter liked me, for once. She made me get my hair streaked, and I was taking dance three times a week that summer. She wanted me to get my nose fixed, too, but my father said no, though I thought he'd used up all his power with her over pilot season. He said general anesthetic was too dangerous and my nose would still be swollen by the time the summer ended.

I overheard my mother say something about "Italian honkers," but to me she said, "Your nose makes you look ethnic, and ethnic is in." I still hated her for it. I know my nose is big, but it's straight and it's not like freaking gigantic. I had learned to put light brown eye shadow down the sides of my nose to make it look narrower and not like it had a big bulb at the end. But I knew she never totally liked how I looked. She would have had me tied to the bumpers of two cars and stretched to make me taller, for one thing. She had these pictures of herself with her sisters in our living room, and they all looked like these tall, thin, beautiful swans with long necks, even in their crappy pink-and-brown seventies clothes. She had three of them framed, one of Maggie, one of her, and one of the three of them. She kept a picture of Marjorie, as the Sugar Plum Fairy in *The Nutcracker*, in a little silver frame in her bedroom. Marjorie was by far the most beautiful. I don't think she thought I looked like one of them. I thought, The hell with her. *Most* actors are really small. I mean, even the guys you think of as big studs are only like five-seven. They just have big photogenic faces, that's all. My coach told me that. The only thing my mother ever liked about me was that I had size six feet and pretty hair. But that came "from her side." The only thing I ever liked about her was nothing. I love her, you know? But I was never good enough. And even stinking drunk, my dad was nicer. Why did she buy me all those clothes? Like, was it to make people think we were rich, which we were, sort of, but not rich like the Gearys or the Neelands, who had what my mother called "family money"? Or did she do it because it was what she would have wanted if she'd been the one going? I left home with four matching tracksuits and four pairs of Nikes, not to mention blazers and long velvet skirts and junk I never even took the tags off.

I got all my ridiculous uniforms—navy blue chinos

with navy blue sweaters and green shorts and skirts—and packed up my clothes. They all had to be embroidered with my name, no name tags or permanent marker.

If I'd known then what would happen to me, I would never have left my room.

IV

I WAS SO READY to be away from home.

I could have had any role I wanted around there, but I wanted a bigger world. I knew that I would kick butt. I knew I had so outgrown Bellamy, in every way. For one thing, I wanted to be around people like me. Acting is a lonely life. You're better than most people at something everyone would do if they could. But it's also just lonely. And it was lonelier for me because I was under my mother's thumb so much I couldn't hang out with kids. I'd never had a boyfriend. Not that I wanted one of the doofs from Bellamy. But I wouldn't have minded them wanting me.

I never had a lot of friends there my own age.

By the time I was in ninth grade, Abby and Hannah from the theater group were the only ones I saw outside rehearsal or school, and then not very much. Abby was a year older and Hannah a year younger. Hannah was totally immature, like calling people and hanging up and TPing houses. But I stayed over probably twice at Hannah's house, even though she also was practically a coach for bulimics and she was gay or doing a pretty good imitation of it. Not that being gay is a bad thing, but she liked me that way, I think. She would sleep next to me in her bed, which was a king-sized bed. And she was close to her family, which I found weird. I knew I had cousins; my aunt Maggie ("the frog dissection queen") had three daughters, and one was my age. She sent me checks at my birthday and Christmas and asked me to come to Denver skiing. I wanted to, but my mother said I would break something. So I hadn't seen my cousins since I was, like, five.

So when Hannah asked me if I would miss seeing my little brother except during summers, I said, "Summers?" Why would I see him in summer?

Who thought I'd be coming home summers? I'd be applying for every possible summer stock thing I could get, if only to get away from my mother. Plus Starwood has a summer program, and if I couldn't get a job, I could talk my dad into letting me go to that. No way was I going back home. I could never have imagined any way Bellamy would look good to me.

Not until now, that is.

Saying good-bye to kids from school was like swatting a mosquito. Too bad, too sad. They never liked me and I never liked them. They hardly ever paid attention to me after fourth grade or so. Especially the ones who were the children of my parents' so-called stuck-up friends.

I hadn't done anything with any of them since I was little. When I was little, some kids would ask me over to play. Or their mothers would. Playdates. What crap. My father wanted me to have a normal social life. Not too much theater—at least until I was about nine or ten.

But he might as well not have bothered. I didn't have anything to say to them. What did they *do* with their lives? Some of them maybe had piano lessons. Or sports. But I had voice, diction, piano, drama, and rehearsal. They had no idea what my life was, so how could we have anything to say to each other?

What they talked about, I totally never got. Video games and toys. Wearing the same color shirt on Fridays! Whippy Skippy! Who liked who and who didn't like somebody anymore, though before they'd been BFFs. It was all so stupid. They didn't even know what the Academy Awards were. They talked about going to Fort Wilderness in Wisconsin Dells for vacation. They had never even been to New York or California. They talked about their brothers and sisters and how irritating or cute they were. I didn't even know what to say back to them. What did you say? They would start doing one thing and five minutes later, it was like, "Want to color?" "Want to see my puppy?" They couldn't stick to anything. They would want to play dolls or swing outside on their swings. I hadn't done baby stuff since I was five; and as for playing outside, I didn't want to get dirty. All my clothes were imported or handmade. Also, I didn't know how to play pretend. I pretended to be other people professionally. I didn't want to draw pictures of me holding my little brother's hand. I probably said six sentences to Carter in my whole life. Like "Merry Christmas" or "Get out of my room." Other kids did stuff with their brothers and sisters. How dull could you be?

It was like I was watching myself playing "child."

It seemed like . . . such a waste of time to be a kid. You know? I never felt like I really was one. I never wanted to be. Carter would get all excited about some science fair at school or some soccer game. And my parents would go, though I could tell they were bored out of their gourds. My mother said she didn't even like being in the same room with women who wore pants with elastic waists.

There was this one time I was basically forced to go

over and "play" with the bigger Neeland girl, Jillian. We watched a dumb Disney show. It was a cartoon, not a show that had kid actors in it that I could maybe learn something from, or see if they were better than me. Then her mother wanted us to make cookies, and Jillian asked could we lick the bowl. I remember saying, "There's a raw egg in that. . . ." Jillian's mother looked at me like I was nuts. But come on, who would want to eat raw dough? I just looked right back at her, while her daughter stuck her fingers in the bowl and licked it until it was all over her hands. So gross, and fattening. Not just because my mother thought so. I mean, once you get used to not eating all that crap, if you really look at it, it's disgusting. I haven't had a real can of pop that wasn't diet since I was six. I didn't want to play video games and go to sleepovers anymore, except with other theater people, and usually not even then. I didn't mind having to wear a cucumber mask and a retainer to bed. I didn't care that I couldn't stay up late like other kids, instead of having to get my ten hours, even on Saturday nights. You *need* ten hours or you look like crap. I *wanted* my hair rolled in those long tendrils even when I was nine. It looked better. I couldn't stand ponytails and French braids that were always coming out. I wasn't pushed. Or at least, I was pushed only until I saw why. After I saw why, no one had to push me.

Look, I was a regular kid. Some mornings, I didn't want to get up at eight and go to rehearsal or lessons. I fought back a little. But it was mostly because I didn't want my mother to think that I was this little puppet who would do anything she said! I don't like anyone controlling me.

Like, when I was little, I used to be embarrassed when my mother would make me sing in front of her company. And she *always* made me sing in front of her company. My dad called her Mama Rose, which was the name of the pushy stage mother in an old musical my mother loved.

But if you don't have a stage mother, you—duh—don't have a career.

At least, at first you don't.

"Oh, sing for us, Bernadettte," my mother would say whenever she got enough people in our house to make up an audience. "Sing, darling! Please." She'd clap her hands. It was pretty stupid.

"Forget it," I would say, even when I was, like, seven, which most people would consider talking back to your mother, but then, they didn't have to deal with my mother's bullshit . . . well, I thought it was bullshit, then. It wasn't until I was eleven, and Annie, that I really got it. It was like she had a magic pill, and when I swallowed it, I saw everything differently.

But not when I was a little kid. I knew her friends thought I was a brat. I also knew that my own mother thought I had a potbelly and a big nose and she still wanted me to be her performing pig. It wasn't like we were all cuddly when no one was around and this was a special thing between us that we loved.

"Please? For Mom?" she would beg. She never gave up, even when she could see I was gritting my teeth and that I just felt so ashamed.

"I said forget it," I would tell her, and I would raise my voice. It was like she couldn't hear. By then the other people would start getting embarrassed. I knew if I held out long enough, she'd sneak me into the screened-in porch and give me five bucks. Maybe ten bucks. I always did it eventually. I did it even when it made me want to crawl under the Oriental rug and flatten out like my brother's hamster, Hammerstein, used to do—until the day our maid vacuumed over him.

There were a few times I totally refused.

But I noticed something. I noticed that if I didn't sing, people just went back to what they were talking about as if I wasn't even there. They were like, "Oh, kids. You know kids." And my mother wouldn't speak to me the whole next day. I hated her, but I hated it worse if she ignored me. So usually I'd do it. I'd get up and sing. I'd sing "When You Wish Upon a Star" or "Where Is

Love?" or one of the other couple of dozen songs my mother laminated and kept in a black binder she called my "repertoire." It wasn't that I liked the way they looked at me. It didn't feel like it did to sing behind footlights, the way it did later. In my own living room, in front of the Weisses and the Schaeffers and Sherry Neeland, the biggest gossip in Bellamy and my mother's so-called best friend, and sometimes even their kids, I felt big and hot and ugly. It was like telling a kid who plays basketball to do a layup in the kitchen "for Mom."

But I just put that thought aside and did it. I'm glad now she never gave up because of just that. It's harder to perform in front of people you know than in front of a thousand strangers, just like it's easier for me to tell Em things about how unfair they were to me than it is to tell my own father. It got me so over performance anxiety that I could have done anything, anywhere, which is how you're supposed to be. Totally loose. For the first few years, I threw up before our Christmas party because I would know that my mother was going to make me sing "Some Children See Him" or "O Holy Night." I dreaded that she was going to ask, but I couldn't wait for her to ask. It was like torture, but it was torture that I started to love. I even started looking forward to the looks of disappointment that perfect Sherry Neeland gave her own kids when I got to the last note of "Stille Nacht" in

German. I would hold the note a little longer.

I would think, She wishes they were as good as me. Her kids were all very average. Average looking. Average in school. Average at sports or whatever they did. They would grow up and live average lives.

Then came eighth grade. And Bellamy was starting to feel like a shirt that didn't button in front anymore. Ninth grade was worse: all these girls standing in groups of five or six, screaming and pretending to fall around laughing, hitting each other, texting each other every five minutes. DUCWIC? Duh. After I got my second national commercial, for a kind of sports shoe, for which I made thousands of dollars, they started calling me "Miss Unpopularity." One of them, Liza Allesandro, even told me, "Not to be mean, but people think it's kind of stuck-up that you have an agent and stuff. You should try to let them know you're a regular person, and then they'll be nicer to you." I sat next to her in math, and I guess she was trying to be nice. She was some kind of weird Christian who believed in "giving."

And I was totally shocked. I said, "I couldn't care less if they include me in stuff!"

But I thought when I went to Starwood, I would have friends. I would have girls like me, who knew what was going on and didn't expect me to act like a "regular person." Then I got there six weeks early, for the summer session, and I was miserable. There were probably only fifty kids there, and hardly any of them were regular students who would be there in the fall. They were not the real talent. More like the kids in the company back home. Not worth wasting my time on them.

The dorms were tacky and cold, and the floors were *linoleum*, and I had to do my own laundry. I had a chore every week. One week it was scraping spaghetti off plates. One week it was making copies of sheet music. Everybody had a rotating roster of chores. I'd never done laundry or dishes in my life! Was this some sort of price you had to pay? They never mentioned scraping off someone's drooly food in the brochure, just cleaning up after yourself and looking well groomed. They told us it was to "instill responsibility," but it was the exact opposite of what being an actor was supposed to be! Which was not having to do any of this crap for yourself. I told my parents. It turned out they *knew* I would have to carry sheets up three flights of stairs! My parents thought the wonderful experience of Starwood would make me be okay with the garbage-y stuff I had to do— stuff I thought would've been done for us by, like, the kind of lunch ladies they had when I was in middle school. Not the paying students! So they didn't tell me.

But no wonderful stuff had started yet! I was just alone, and everyone else was an idiot. And I was scraping plates and had a tiny six-line part in some modern psycho play a former student wrote about people getting shot in an airport. I played a girl who couldn't find a cab. About thirty people showed up for it.

The first semester started. And then, instead of really being nice to a new kid, everyone knew each other because they'd all gone there since seventh grade, and they all ignored me.

I wanted to go home—even to Bellamy—but my parents made me promise I would stay the whole first semester because they already paid up front and it was a lot and I would get used to it.

The first weeks were horrible! The choral director told me to stop shouting—that the object was to complement each other's voices, not drown each other out. No one had ever said anything like that to me before. I think she just hated me because she was so freaking ugly and old. But she said I was probably used to "local" vocal groups where the standards were much lower. I almost died. I was going to just walk out, but people stared at me like only a freak would do that. I went back to my place. I was going to get on a bus and leave that night.

When I called my mother, she said, "Bernadette. Hope. You listen to me. Your brother had to go to public school to give you this chance. . . ."

"Uh, this is me, not caring," I said.

"I don't care if you don't care," she yelled at me. "Go back there and do what they tell you! This isn't the first time in your life you've ever been corrected. . . ."

"It is the first time by some ninety-year-old idiot who tells stories about how she was in the original production of *Hair*!" I said. "In front of a whole bunch of kids who can't probably do this stuff as good as I do it! I can't stand it."

"You can stand anything. And plus, I'm not paying for you to come back, so lump it," she said, and she hung up. She sent me a hundred dollars by FedEx. I bought all these scented pens and junk.

And then it came to me.

One night, when I was practicing signing my name different ways. It came to me.

Why kids were ignoring me, and being so obvious about it. Why the teachers in dance class were like, "Didn't you learn a double pirouette by now? Did you really study ballet?" And the teachers in English were like, "You don't know what 'observational' means?"

It was this. They had never seen anyone like me. They were jealous. The other kids were there for an education along with acting. I was just there to make it to the next level. Even though a lot of the girls were beautiful and clique-y, they didn't have what I had! I called my mother and asked her if she thought I was right, and she said, Of course, people were always going to be jealous of the best one, and hadn't she always said that? I started crying and said yes, but that I didn't know how brave you had to be. She said the good stuff is always hard. Someone came up to the phone booth—kids weren't allowed cell phones until junior year—and asked if I was all right and I had to tell them to screw off.

My mother said, "Do something different. Make them want you. And think beyond Starwood. There are agents who come to see those shows all the time. What if they're looking for a particular type, all over the country? What if a big agent sees you and you're at your best? You could end up leaving there for a movie. I bet you don't even get to graduate." I knew that she was right about this, at least.

So I started by starving until I was almost the thinnest girl at Starwood, practically, except for a couple of dancers. I had cheekbones that stuck out and made me look like photos of old movie stars. I studied Audrey Hepburn's clothes and started wearing big sunglasses and capri pants and flat shoes on our "free day Fridays" and on weekends. I would just sit and stare in the mirror and measure how much thinner my face was every day. I was so skinny I looked sick, but sick in a beautiful way. They even asked to see me in the infirmary. But there was nothing wrong with me. I thought quickly and said

I had just started running and I hadn't really done any hard exercise before, plus I was getting taller. They wanted me to come back after Thanksgiving to be checked, or they would contact my parents. Like my parents would have cared! My mom was giving me StarCaps when I was twelve! I knew enough not to get creepy, insect thin. When I got famous, I didn't want to end up in magazines for being thin. So I walked this fine line. I looked in library books about the Oscars. I was sort of a dark-haired Gwyneth Whatever-Her-Name-Is. Like Keira Knightley, but dark-skinned. I had seen some of those Oscar movies. Most of them my mother had to make me watch; but then, it made sense why she wanted me to see them. I would be able to do comedy like that, like, so moving that it would make you cry. I would do tragedy so sly you could laugh. I would make all the stars in *People* look like dogs, but I would be womanly, too, and mysterious. The perfect combination of all of them. Not some teenybopper in cute movies about single dads with daughters who were twins.

Real films.

So that's what I started getting ready for.

My break.

I was sure it would come as soon as I got my first real role.

I ordered forty monologue books with my mom's

credit card, and I started memorizing. After all, I only had to pass the other classes, not ace them. And they were easy. Science but not real science. Just enough so you weren't a moron. My parents would have me tutored for the college entrance exams and have someone write the essay for me. Eating got to be something I didn't even want to do. One night, totally out of the blue, Carter, my brother, called me. He was like, "Are you all right?" and I was like, "Whatever." I said, "How are you?" He said he was good. I was nice to him because I was that lonely. But I pushed it down. I was on a total quest.

Then, a lightning bolt hit the ground next to me.

I saw Logan for the first time in the cafeteria, where I was picking at my salad, sitting alone at one of the long wooden tables. He had just come to the school for his senior year, even though he'd already done a couple of guest appearances on a TV show. He came into the room like he was making an entrance, for which I didn't blame him, and even the guys looked up. He wasn't tall or big, but he made you feel he was tall and big and powerful. He scanned the whole room, with his hands stuck in the pockets of his old leather bomber jacket. And then he started across the room. Toward me! He came and swung his leg over the bench and sat down beside me! My breath started to come faster until I was almost dizzy.

But I told myself, Keep your thoughts straight. Stay in the center.

"What would you say if I told you that you were beautiful, kiddo?" he asked. And like, I know that was a line. But who cares?

I said, "I'd tell you that you were probably smart. And dumb. I might be beautiful. But you don't just come up and tell a girl that."

"Exotic."

"Just different."

"Beyond different."

"It's your call."

"Then I'm calling it," he said, and starting eating my cherry tomatoes.

It was like lines from a movie, and we were the stars. That natural and completely perfect. You don't usually have a moment like that.

For the first time I knew why they call it being hit by an arrow through your heart when you fall in love. Go back and look at the beginning of this journal entry. Look at those Roman numerals. The IV. That doesn't mean "intravenous." That's me, lonely, yes, but brave and thin and alone, glamorous in being alone. And then suddenly, there's Logan. The arrow. There he is. And everything changes. I look into his gigantic green eyes, almost like fake eyes, with lashes longer than mine. And I'm shot through the heart. "He jests at scars that never felt a wound," says Romeo, right before the balcony scene. You might laugh, but I knew this was it. My whole life was going to change forever. And it did. I was a woman. Even before anything happened between us.

He was so beautiful.

He didn't have one single zit.

I still love him, if you can believe that.

V

THERE HE IS, at the top of my journal entry, the arrow that cut through my soul.

Look, I knew it wasn't a little crush.

A woman can tell. I was more mature for my age. He knew I was mature for my age too. And our love was like a storm, so big it knocked us both over. I had never even been kissed before, much less done the sickening stuff some of the girls in Bellamy did, like get drunk and let the neighbor kid climb in the window and feel you up. I had never wanted some acne-face slob's hands all over me after he was done picking his pimples. Logan was so pure. He smelled pure, like pine. And how do you know it's love when you were never in love before? Well, I had seen love in the movies and on the stage. And you know how the follow spotlight just narrows down until it's only shining on one person? That's what love is like. The whole world fades until you can only hear that person's voice and see that person's face. No matter who he's pretending to talk to, you know he's talking to you, that he wants you to hear. And when he crosses the room, even if he's teasing and pretending he doesn't see you, there's this connection. You both feel it. You know he's been thinking about you since the last time he saw you and you've been thinking about him, totally nonstop. I could get physically sick and not be able to eat just thinking about him. At night, in bed, every song on the radio would be him, singing to me. I would think of him out there, in his room, looking out the window and wanting me, and I could hardly stand it. Logan was my breath. I needed him from the first moment. Needed him. We used to try not to look at each other—after all, I was just a kid and he was almost nineteen. People would have said stuff and totally been jealous. He *was* Logan Rose. And we were probably too far apart in age, maybe. Maybe a little. But we couldn't stop. Wherever I would go, there he would be. I would be sitting on the floor outside the choral room reading and he'd be coming out of class and he'd practically trip over me, and I knew he wanted to grab me up right there—but he would just kind of laugh and mess up my hair and go jogging off with a bunch of guys. Once, when one of them said, "There's your shadow," he punched the guy on the shoulder. He didn't want to hear that about me.

I knew it was the kind of love that would last if the world would not mess it up.

It wasn't like he started going after me the first minute. There was that little thing in the cafeteria his first day. But then he was totally cool about it, and so was I. But he would do this thing. He would sort of stop like he had been hit on the back of the head when he passed me (freshman and sophomores had to march in lines across the road from our dorms to class; it was part of the big security thing) and act like he'd never seen me before that very moment. He would act like it made his day.

Tryouts for *Romeo and Juliet* were coming up.

I had read the play in eighth grade and ninth grade, but I read it again twice.

Everyone knew Romeo was Logan. It was a done deal. And the tradition was that Starwood always had a guest director for the winter play. This time it was Brook Emerson.

The students were going totally nuts. Usually it was some over-the-hill person, but Brook Emerson had won a Tony just two years before for playing Antonio in *The Feast of Fools*, which I personally thought was one of those talky-talky musicals that doesn't have one single song in it anyone will ever remember, but people really loved it, I guess.

All the girls were practicing monologues. The first thing you had to do was just a one-minute thing, not from Shakespeare. We knew all the major roles would go to the seniors, because directors and scouts from colleges came to the winter play too. But that didn't stop anyone from trying out. There were going to be plenty of street guys and waiting maids or whatever, and any of us would have been glad to be one of them. I just wanted to stand on the same stage as Logan.

But then, there was this one girl I started to notice in French class. Alyssa. Alyssa Lyn Davore. She was like the red-haired girl who should've been Annie instead of me. She *was* Juliet, with long sandy hair that hung below her waist. Alyssa reminded me of a candle, she was so pale and almost transparent. And though she was a dancer, she could really act in a semi-phony kind of way, which works with Shakespeare. Her father was an English professor, so she didn't have to have anyone explain stuff to her. She knew how to place her hands like they were little statues. Do you ever notice actors' hands? How they don't just let them hang by their sides or stick them in their pockets? They pose their hands. Their hands are like little speaking voices, saying something to the audience. Plus, Alyssa Lyn was a junior. And I thought if any underclass person got to be Juliet, it would be her.

I tried to take some hope from the fact that Juliet

was Italian, like me.

But northern Italians are blond.

We had tryouts on a Wednesday, starting right after lunch, in the big theater. Classes were canceled for the afternoon. Even the little eighth graders came to watch.

Brook explained the play to us, like anyone who hadn't been in prison all their life wouldn't know what *Romeo and Juliet* was. He talked about its relevance to life now, about class and racial hatred, and how kids would be the ones who would start the healing. I felt like I was going to yawn, so I pretended to fix something on my shoe.

Then we all did our one-minute monologues.

I did the scene from *Our Town* that got me into Starwood. Other girls did monologues from monologue books, like about not wanting to clean your room or whatever. Like that would so impress Brook Emerson.

Then they started little readings, from the actual script. Brook started out with the scene where everyone's teasing Romeo for falling around like an idiot because he's so in love—like the way Logan tripped over me. And then there's the big fight between Romeo's cousins and some guys who are Capulet guys and such.

Those were the parts most of the guys read for.

A few guys read for Romeo, and one really good senior read for Mercutio and Romeo.

But then, the director basically lined up girls to read Juliet with Logan. Like, twenty girls. I was almost the last one. I decided to do the most familiar scene, but in a new way. The part where she asks, "Wherefore art thou Romeo?" But I acted really pissed off, like a real fourteen-year-old girl would, a rich girl having a tantrum because her boyfriend's retard family was so into being Montagues. I drew on changing my own name, and how it felt weird but free, when I told him to leave his family and forsake his name. I did it like she wasn't pleading, but she was ripping him a new one.

They let us break for dinner; and then he put the call-back list outside the big hall.

They had called five girls back.

Alyssa Lyn was one, and there were three seniors. And me.

When I came back into the hall, Brook Emerson sat me down. He said, "I don't think I ever saw that scene played that way. Who told you to do it that way?"

I said no one. I just thought about her really being my age—I had just turned fifteen—and how fifteen-year-old girls really act, which is like they have the world by the . . . I almost said "balls" but said "tail" in time—especially if they're cute and have a boy they love.

He said, "You remind me of the young Gwyneth Paltrow, except for the hair. Or Natalie Portman. With a little Drew Barrymore and maybe Anne Hathaway." Those weren't the actors you saw on *People* magazine covers. They were actors in real movies. They were kind of old, but they were still beautiful.

I was about to jump out of my skin. I couldn't believe he saw that! It was true, but nobody else ever saw that before but me.

The four other girls read. He thanked them and he said he would post his final choices on the board outside in the morning. He said that callbacks for Lady Capulet and the Nurse and such would be the next night.

He asked everyone else to leave. I didn't know what was going on, because this was so unlike any other audition I ever did.

I could see Alyssa Lyn looking at me like she wished I would catch on fire. But when she read with Logan, it just didn't go snap, crackle, pop. She sounded limp, like she was already dead. And she sort of looked dead too, when the lights were on her. Pale is great for makeup, but not so much when you don't have it on. I could see Brook scribbling in his notebook. He kept asking her to go over the same scene again and again. I started praying to Catholic saints. Finally he told her she could sit down.

And then he had me and Logan read the scene where Romeo and Juliet are secretly married and they slept together, but he has to run away the next morning for killing the guy in the street fight, and Juliet says, "Wilt thou be gone? It is not yet near day. It was the nightingale, and not the lark. . . ." I let myself go, and my teeth started chattering and chattering. I was stuttering like you would if you were in a panic. "'Yon light is not d-d-day-light, I know it; I. It is some meteor. . . .'" And then I screamed when I said, "'Thou need'st not to be gone!'"

And Logan sort of grabbed me and said, in this way that was almost angry and totally sexy, "'Let me be ta'en, let me be put to death, I am content, so thou wilt have it so.'"

We basically forgot Brook was there. We got so into it we were standing there, and Logan was putting his hands all over my neck and my bare arms, and kissing my throat when I put my head back.

Finally Brook said, "Jesus Christ. Tone it down. I'll get arrested."

I looked out at him, and it was like waking up from a dream.

"You've got it," he said like someone had hit him. "I couldn't let anyone else be Juliet, or I would be untrue to myself. I'm going to catch hell for it, though, because you're just a kid, so you'd better not let me down, or I'll kick your ass." I promised I wouldn't let him down. "Alyssa Lyn can do one of the school shows. Jesus! I never saw chemistry like this on a first read."

Logan said, "It's been there all along, since the first time I saw her."

I felt like I was flying.

Brook got up and said, "I think we have our star-crossed lovers." He took off his glasses and said to Logan, "I know you can handle it. But she's a sophomore, Logan."

Logan said, "She's been doing this longer than most of the girls here."

Brook got up and shut off the lights on the stage then, and said to us, "Go out the back way. If you run into any faculty, I'm going to have to explain this, and I just don't feel like it right now. I have to make about fifty phone calls tonight. To my agent and whoever." Logan told him that he could walk me home because he was an SA. Brook said that was okay. An SA was a Senior Achiever, one of the older students who could go anywhere they wanted, even at night, and who were the escorts for younger students who couldn't. So I guess Brook felt fine about leaving us alone, because of that. And the back door would be closer to the dorms.

Brook said, "No funny stuff." Logan laughed like they were both adults. "Turn out the lights. The main switch is right by the stage door."

Then he put on his coat and picked up his clipboard and left. I heard the door lock, and then I heard the outside glass door swish.

I put on my coat. Logan didn't put on his coat, though. I put on my leather gloves. Logan just watched me, with those huge green eyes, like lakes or moons. He was sitting on a metal stool in the middle of the stage. I flipped my hair out of the collar of my coat. Logan said, "Did you ever cut your hair?"

I said, "Just the ends."

He said, "You have the most beautiful hair I have ever seen."

I sort of blushed. I said, "Thank you."

Logan asked me, "Do you really want to go back to the dorms?"

I said, kind of desperately, "Of course I don't! But everyone knows tryouts are over, and my dorm advisor will kill me."

He said, "Just let me take care of your dorm advisor." Then he said, "You know how I feel about you, Hope."

I said, "I feel the same way. But what are we going to do about it? We're here, and everyone knows who you are. And I'm just this kid from Bellamy, Illinois. . . ."

"Not really," he said. "You're the real thing, Hope. Most of these girls will never make it after they leave here. But let's forget about acting right now, and concentrate on us."

My heart was so loud, I was sure if you pulled up my

shirt you could see the outline of it under my skin, pounding. I started to walk toward the wings, like I really was going to leave. If he didn't *do something* fast, I was going to completely lose it. The emotions between us were like the fake fog they use in the theater for scary stuff. It's really just dry ice. But it was like it was rising and rising and it was going to cover us both up. I said, "Logan, don't do anything you can't take back. I'm really like Juliet. I've never loved anyone but you."

Then Logan said, "But halt. . . ," and he took me by the hand and led me into the wings. Then he lowered me down on my back on a pile of the old curtains that had just been taken down and left on the stage. He unbuttoned my coat and sweater as gently as he could.

And that was when we did it, for the first time.

People say your first time is always awful, but mine was totally natural and it was totally exciting. I had never even kissed a boy. I never wanted to. They were all so gross, sweating and farting and sickening when they ate. And I was already so charged up from getting the part that every inch of my skin felt like it had a separate candle burning under it, so when he reached up and slipped off my bra, I didn't even think to stop him. We were like one person, and it didn't even hurt, the way other girls said it did. It was like we were two beautiful spirits who had our own world all to ourselves, and I knew this would be the only time I would feel this way or he would feel this way. I don't know if it took minutes or, like, hours. You don't think of time when you're with someone you love. It's just like you want to study every part of that person's face and hands and his chest and everything. He looked like some magazine ad for Dolce & Gabbana, like if it weren't dark, he would be sun-tanned, posing on the deck of a ship. And I would be there too, just as beautiful, his perfect match. I loved Logan. I totally, completely loved Logan, and when I let him make love to me, I knew it was something we didn't even need words for. And I totally trusted that he would never tell anyone. He would protect me, because telling anyone would make it seem like I was a slut.

When we were *finally* dressed, he didn't walk me home. He put my coat around my shoulders, and we went out to his car. He drove me to town. He had his own car, because seniors were allowed. We went to Chatters, and we ate.

Logan said, "You know that meant something to me. I hope you didn't think I was just trying to take advantage of the moment. I hope it meant something to you, too. I don't want it to be something that ends."

"I wouldn't have done it if I hadn't wanted to," I said, but I was starting to freak out a little. I was starting to realize that, just like Juliet, I had given my virginity to a guy right away. If it hadn't been Logan, I would have been scared. I said, "I don't ever want it to end."

It was close to midnight when we got back, and Lisa, my dorm advisor, had to unlock the door. She came swooping down on us like this big spider.

"Brook Emerson kept us late," Logan told her. I didn't say anything. I was sure she could see it all over me, what we'd done. It's true. You do look different, and I could see how jealous she was.

Lisa was probably in her twenties, really a lot older, but she was all over Logan. She asked, "Are you Logan Rose?" and Logan was like, yeah, sort of humble, and Lisa said, "I saw you in *Miss Fortune*. I think it's cool that you're finishing school here."

He said, "People who don't finish are stupid. They end up zoners half the time."

Lisa asked, "Are you going to college or right to L.A.?"

"College. If they'll have me. There are no guarantees in the business," he said.

"Yeah, but you've already been in a movie and on TV," she was saying, all gushy. "You know you could go to any college." He just sort of nodded. "Would you take a year off if you got a part in a movie?" He nodded again. "That's totally understandable," Lisa said.

She would have gone on talking all night, and I just

wanted to be alone in my room and relive the whole thing, and I knew Logan did too, so I started to squeeze past her and go upstairs so my poor Logan could finally leave. Lisa said then, "Hope. Your mother called, like, ten times, and I didn't know what to tell her. You'll have to be written up. . . ."

"You won't write her up," Logan pleaded, getting down on his knees. "Blame me. Write me up." Lisa blushed like she was my age or something. Logan knew what to do in any situation.

"Well, not this time."

I ran upstairs and tore off my clothes. I was going to jump in the shower like I always did, but who would want to wash Logan away? Then I opened my window and leaned out so my cell phone semi-worked and called my mother. Okay, so I wasn't supposed to have a cell. But it was a stupid rule.

"What the hell is going on?" she yelled at me. "It's one in the morning! Tryouts were over at nine!"

"I had to stay late, and Mom, there was this guy." I had to make something up fast. "It was when I was crossing the road, and he followed me in his truck, and we had to run—"

"We, who's we?" she asked. "What do you mean, followed you?"

"Like in a creepy way. And 'we' was Logan Rose.

82

Mom, he's been in a movie with Ben Stiller and he's been on *Wailea Alive* and he's eighteen and he likes me. He's here to finish senior year, and he's going to be Romeo."

"Oh," she said, and I could hear the excitement in her voice. "He likes you, like, a girlfriend?"

"Yes, but that's not all." I paused and breathed in the moonlight. "Mom, I got Juliet."

"Oh my God, Hope." She started to cry. I could hear her yelling for my father, and him in the background, all slurring, obviously having had his customary four "dirty" martinis. Him saying, "Way to go, Bernadette!" "You mean, they didn't give it to a senior?"

"No, me! Well, there's this one girl who'll probably do some of the shows. But she's sort of my understudy. . . ."

"Oh, Hopie! I never would have believed this was possible!"

"Well, believe it!"

"You'll have to get your hair streaked again!"

"Mom, Juliet didn't have highlights! He likes it black—Brook Emerson!"

"Oh my God! Mark! It's Brook Emerson. From *Feast of Fools*! That's the guest director. When do you start rehearsals? Now remember, no white food between now and then. No bread. No milk . . ."

"Mom! I know how to do this," I said. I wanted to get

off the phone. My beautiful dream was fading. I had to think about it, feel it, let it come back to life. "I have to get to sleep, Mom," I began.

Then she asked, "Did you tell your friend, Levon . . ."

"Logan . . ."

"Or your advisor, or whatever she is? About the guy on the road?"

I was actually relieved. She was totally off the track. If I had been older, or if we had been closer, I could have told her that I just had the most totally emotional time of my life. I could never tell her. Not now or two years from now. She'd have pulled me out of Starwood so fast, I wouldn't have had time to grab my toothbrush. Or maybe not. If she thought it was somebody who could get me someplace, maybe she would have been almost okay with it. Knowing my mom, she'd have sent me a care package with chocolate chip cookies and condoms.

VI

LOGAN AND ME.

That was my whole world.

Logan and me.

See my journal heading up there, for today? I haven't actually written anything for two weeks because I've been too tired and busy with homework crap. But there it is. The arrow that pierced my heart and me. Side by side, always.

Logan.

And me.

It was a week until rehearsal began. I hadn't seen Logan. Not that we were avoiding each other, or anything. When I did see him, for the first read-through, I sort of blushed. But once rehearsals began, it was as if we had been together for our whole lives. As if there were nothing we couldn't tell each other. And we were together constantly, every moment that we weren't in class or in public.

By "in public," I mean we didn't eat lunch together or dinner or anything, because people would have started talking. That was my idea. I didn't want to be gossiped about. People were jealous enough.

When the casting was announced, a couple of the senior girls actually started to cry and ran out of the hall. This big, mean blond girl who'd played Rizzo in *Grease* the year before said, "Bite me on the leg and call me Rover. That little shit! I can't believe it!" As if they were going to cast some big fat chick as Juliet. I'm so sure. She was lucky to get in at all, as Juliet's mother. That's not a bad role.

I did what my mother said and kept my head low.

"People are going to be jealous of you your whole life," she said when I called to tell her she needed to send me a bunch of new rehearsal clothes. I was using Brook's cell and I put Logan on. He was a little shy, but he said, "Uh, hi, Mrs. Romano."

I could hear my mom. "'Romeo, Romeo, wherefore art thou Romeo'?" she asked, like she didn't even know that "wherefore" meant "why."

Later Logan told me his mom was mostly the same way. "It must be genetic," he said. "You know, like those pillows that say anyone can be a father, but it takes someone special to be a dad? Well, anyone can be a good mom, but it takes someone special to be a stage mother." I laughed so hard I had to stop running and catch my breath.

We went running together a lot, and then afterward we made love outside. Or else we would go to this little broken-down hunter's cabin where the seniors went to drink. There were blankets there and a bathroom with running water. It was cold, but there was a woodstove, and once we started it and stayed for hours.

Logan wasn't allowed to come into my dorm room. And I wasn't allowed in the guys' dorm, either.

It was hard for us.

Like, there was the time we mutually decided that he would take the big blonde, Grace Carnahan, to Homecoming. Logan didn't want people to think that we were together the way we were. It would have looked bad for me. I might have gotten kicked out of school. You weren't supposed to date other students—well, have a sexual relationship at school—even if you were the same age. And definitely not a senior with a sophomore.

And plus, we were starting to talk about The Plan.

Logan brought it up one night when we were lying on the sleeping bag together at the cabin.

"I can't stand the idea of leaving you next year," he said. "You're like the whole world to me, Hope. I can't imagine living without you."

"But what are we going to do, then?" I asked. "I have two more years here, and then college."

"Well, we could skip out," he said. "We could just run away, you and me. We could work as waiters until we got work in movies or on Broadway and then when you're twenty-one, we could get married."

I was totally over the sun and the moon, then. Logan was asking me to marry him! It was a big decision—a big decision to make at fifteen. But I knew he was the one. It's like our futures were, like, entwined—we knew we were fated to be together. So I kissed him very softly and said, "Yes, a thousand times yes! I'll go with you anywhere on Earth, Logan."

So then we really had to start being careful. We couldn't let anyone suspect we were together. Can you imagine how that felt? We practically had to act like we weren't even friends: "Hi, Logan." "Hi, Hope." If I was going to take off with Logan when he graduated, I didn't want it to get around that we were in love now. My parents would kill me, and the school would be responsible for their most famous student—well, after the play their two most famous students—sleeping together.

What Logan explained to me was this: he was going to go to college in the fall, but at Michigan, not at Carnegie Mellon in Pittsburgh, so he could be near me.

Then, when I turned sixteen, in junior year? I was going to quit. We were going to go to L.A. or New York, take his car, use up the credit cards, take out all the money in my account, and just go! My parents would freak, but I'd tell them I was going to go to Stella Adler or the Actors Studio. I could talk them into that, especially if I let them pay for a room at one of those "girl dorms" where acting students live, even if I really, secretly lived with Logan.

I couldn't believe that in a year, I would be living with Logan, waking up with him every morning, making his coffee, walking to the subway with him and holding his hand, and he'd be coming home every night if he didn't have a rehearsal and the two of us would have a candlelight dinner. Okay, it might only be rice and beans, but it would be by candlelight! We would live way up on the West Side, or some other cheap place, as long as we could live together. Maybe we would get a big German shepherd. I imagined us walking the dog together on Sunday mornings in Riverside Park, drinking our Starbucks. I imagined Logan tackling me so he could cover me up with leaves and then us making out on the grass on some warm fall day. You probably think it was crazy for a fifteen-year-old to be thinking like this. But I wasn't any fifteen-year-old. And it's different with people in the business. You grow up faster. You can make decisions better because you've had to make so many decisions on the stage that had an effect on your future, because every performance affects your future.

Anyway, you can tell that Logan and I knew we had something that was probably unique in the world—like the real Romeo and Juliet. I know that sounds nuts. But they knew even though they were made-up people. Logan and I didn't even have to talk to each other every day to totally maintain our connection. What we said with our eyes, at rehearsal, was more than most people say to each other their whole lives with their stupid mouths. I basically lived for rehearsals, and our times alone in the woods. Then we could hold each other close and talk about The Plan. How good the bagels would be in New York. How we could go to the beach in L.A. How it wouldn't take long to get work. I could do Disney and Nickelodeon things: I was so small I could still play a kid. So Florida was another option. I started subscribing to the casting magazine *Stage Door*, for both L.A. and New York, and looking for paying roles that might be suitable for me or Logan. I cut them out and slipped them through the slots in his mailbox, and I would watch, hiding myself just for fun, as he took them out and pretended to be all puzzled.

I wish we had just stuck to The Plan.

The Idea messed up The Plan. Alyssa Lyn must have

had something to do with it. Because the Logan I knew, my Logan, would never have double-crossed me that way. Now I realize that the minute that The Idea was born, The Plan, and our love, started to die.

But I didn't know that yet. Rehearsals went on, and I never got any bad notes. (Notes, if you don't know, are things the director writes down when you're rehearsing. Like "We can't see you in scene two, act one, because you're turned the wrong way" or "The emphasis has to be on 'grave' man. It's a joke, but it's also a pun. He knows he's going to die.") You get sometimes a whole page of those sentences, and they hurt. You get them after a rehearsal, and you have to fix the things you did wrong or you get in trouble, or even out of the show, replaced by somebody else. Brook was super-critical of Alyssa Lyn, saying, "You're going to be out there in two weeks. Out there! And I don't see that you've taken this to your soul! And I don't want to see you play Juliet, and I don't care if you have before; I want you to *be* Juliet. Like, I'm not seeing desperation in the scene where she's begging the Nurse. I need to see panic. This girl is about to lose her mind!" She spent a lot more time onstage than I did, but that was just because she wasn't as good. I would just sit in my seat, smug as the cat who got the cream, waiting for my turn to show her how they did it *downtown* (and I don't mean downtown Black Sparrow

Lake, Michigan). I never got notes, not once. Brook just kept saying, "Very fresh. Very fresh. Follow that, Hope. . . ." almost like he was distracted, because I didn't really need direction; and then he would give pages of notes to everybody else. You could tell Alyssa Lyn was jealous, because she started mocking me.

This one time? I was in the lounge reading, and there was this guy, Brent Sawyer, sitting in one of the big armchairs. His girlfriend was sitting on the chair, sort of fooling with his hair, the way I always sat on the arm of a chair with Logan. She was clearly imitating us. Logan was studying at a table by the fireplace. Then Alyssa Lyn and her best friend, Monique, came in. "There she is," Alyssa said. "She clings to him like the fabric softener sheets cling to the ass of my pants."

"I'd like to put the toe of my boot up her ass," Monique said, loud enough for anyone to hear. "She thinks she's so all that."

"She has no ass!" Alyssa said, and the two of them collapsed all over each other the way the idiots back in Bellamy used to, like what they said was so, so funny. "Logan!" Alyssa called then. "Can you come outside just for a minute? I have something to show you." She said it all sexy. That was one of the times I really hated being secret the most. I would have so loved to tell her Logan was *mine*.

He played along, though. He got up and followed Alyssa Lyn, but he turned back and shrugged and winked at me.

At least nothing could spoil our joy in working together. When we rehearsed the death scenes, Brook closed the set. It was just Logan and me. (And Alyssa Lyn. And once in a while, Logan's understudy.)

If I loved Logan before, I loved him even more when he sat down on the boards they had set up on a sawhorse as the stone bench Juliet lies down on in the crypt, and let his head drop into his hands. He had a new way he wanted to do the famous scene where Romeo finds Juliet dead and decides he has to kill himself with poison to be with her. She thought he was dead and that was why she killed herself . . . it's all very confused, but people in Shakespeare are always doing stuff because they think another person did something that they really didn't do. Anyhow, Logan hesitated so long that Brook almost said something, but just at the last moment, he let his hand trail down my face and my body, between my breasts, as if he were feeling for my heartbeat. He said, "Here's to my love!" He began to laugh, this sad, awful laugh; it was unbelievable. "O true apothecary! Thy drugs are quick. Thus with a kiss I die." And he shrugged, like a kid would do, and grabbed his stomach and made a lot of sort of gagging noise and fell to his knees, all curled up.

Brook said, "Do you think that's over the top?"

Logan got up and said, "You're the boss. But I studied it. And this stuff he would have swallowed, it hurts. It burns. He'd have trouble talking. It's not like you just fall asleep. They make the dagger scene so pretty too. But you know how hard you have to push to stab yourself? She'd be huffing like a choo-choo train."

Brook said, "Good point." He laughed. "Just a . . . little less gagging? But the rest of it, okay. . . ."

The great part for me was that I didn't have to act. I *was* Logan's love, and he was mine. Like once, I passed Logan with The Big Blonde. I remember it was snowing and they had to put off the big bonfire that the school had in the fall every year, so people were kind of down because it was supposedly a lot of fun, a lot of people performing and singing and stuff. Logan had his arm around The Big Blonde, but he winked at me, and said, "Hey, Shortie! 'A greater power than we can contradict Hath thwarted our intents'!" Anyone who didn't know would have thought he meant the bonfire and was just using a line from *Romeo and Juliet*. But I knew it was meant as a message for me, that we couldn't let anyone know, that he didn't really want to be with her. It was all for the sake of appearances. I understood; it was torture, seeing him walk around like he was a player, and then having to forgive him when he was lying in my arms. I would tell him how much it hurt, and he would ask me, "Why do you let it get to you? Why don't you just blow it off?"

He just couldn't get it. He had all those friends. I just had him. I really had hoped that the people at Starwood would turn out to be mature enough that I could be friends with them. They turned out to be just as stupid as the people back home. By Halloween I knew people suspected Logan and I were going out, because the mocking got worse. Other girls would pass me and burst out laughing, because I have this habit of repeating my lines when I'm walking along. They made fun of it instead of respecting it. Once Alyssa Lyn, that bitch, said, "Are you getting any answers back from whoever you're talking to, Hope?" I just ignored them. But it wasn't easy.

I had to remember that in just a year, Logan and I would be together. I would think of us as being one of those power couples on the red carpet, with every girl wanting to be her and every guy wanting to be him.

And that was why I went along with it when he suggested The Idea. That, and I knew he loved me more than anything on Earth. Logan said we couldn't be sure that we'd be able to afford to live only working in restaurants. Big cities are expensive! And if my parents had some objection, and they really stuck to it, what would we do? Logan's parents were going to be pissed off about him dropping out of college unless it was for a movie role. We both knew that in time, our parents would come around. But coming back would not be an option. It would be absolutely unacceptable. Logan was worried about what we would do when we first got there. That was what led to The Idea. That, and how furious I got at Logan for getting *me* in trouble at Homecoming!

That night, I was supposed to wait for him to come to my room after the dance. He would sneak in, as I'd snuck out five or six times before. I spent Homecoming night sitting in my room, trying not to give in and eat a whole bag of Twix my mother had sent. (My costume had a twenty-two-inch waist. I didn't dare eat anything.) I had to stay awake. I knew he would come to me after the dance. So I kept taking off my makeup and putting it on until three in the morning, going down and checking the door, because I had stuck a folded piece of cardboard in it so the alarm wouldn't go off when Logan came.

But he never showed up, and Lisa found the cardboard in the door just when I was coming down to check for Logan. Because I'm an honest person, I admitted that I had been the one who put it there.

Lisa *said* it wasn't a big deal because I really hadn't done anything, only planned to. But then, she made a report! I got written up for putting the cardboard in the door. I had to go to the girls' dean, Miss Lobelier, and be given the third degree.

"What was the purpose of trying to defeat the security system, Hope?" she kept asking me.

"I just like to go out at night sometimes. It helps me think. And it's totally safe here. You know, there's no one around," I said.

"Hope, we have a security system for a reason. It's not to keep our students in. It's to keep others out."

"I know. But I'm not used to so many rules," I said.

"Hope, three serious write-ups means dismissal," said Miss Lobelier, looking down her big nose at me over her half lenses. "I'm going to have to tell your parents about this in a formal letter."

"They'll take me out," I said. "They're very protective. They'll make me leave immediately."

I thought this would stop her: I mean, losing Juliet? And why was she freaking crazy over a nothing little event? She had to know that kids went out to the cabin and drank, practically every night! I was going to say that, when I realized maybe it was not such a good idea because Logan and I went there too. So I put on the sweetness. I said that I really wasn't going to go anywhere. I said I never go anywhere. I said I was getting straight As and the only place I ever went was rehearsal.

I just wanted to go outside and stretch or maybe run. I used to run at night all the time at home, I told her, hoping she wouldn't ask me if I went running at three in the morning. "I was kind of depressed," I said. "Because everyone else went to Homecoming." Lobelier's face seemed to twitch a little. Maybe it was a smile.

"I can't bend the rules for anyone," she said, and I could already tell that she was going to do just that. She sighed and leaned back in her chair. I could, like, read her thoughts. She was thinking why did she want to cause all this trouble for a kid who was just lonely and wishing she was at the big dance (like I sooooo cared!). She was thinking about all the people who would be coming to the play and that Brook Emerson would throw a total tantrum if he had to recast. Adults really have no morals. They just pretend they're going to stick to something, but they always cave in if it's going to look bad for them.

But, hey, I was furious. That night at the rehearsal, when I got to the "wherefore art thou Romeo" part, I was practically spitting at Logan. Brook told me to tone it down. Logan sort of hung his head. Then I practically ate the girl alive who was playing the Nurse when she told me that Romeo had killed Tybalt. "'O serpent heart, hid with a flow'ring face!'" I cried out at her, raising my hand as if I would slap her, treating her like a rich girl really would treat a servant who brought her bad news.

"'Beautiful tyrant! Fiend angelical!'" I made sure that Logan could see my face from the wings. Brook said I was overwhelming in my power.

"Just like the spoiled brat Juliet would be," he said, clapping his hands.

Later on that night, Logan was holding me and kept trying to get me to kiss him, but I wouldn't. He apologized ten times. I just kept pulling away. We were standing down by the boathouse, where nobody could see us. It wasn't curfew yet. We'd gotten done early that night. I said, "Look. You say you love me. You have me, body and soul. You want me to go away with you and spend my life with you. And then you just don't show up and I get in trouble. You so spent the night with that . . . sow. I know you did!"

"Look," he said finally. "This is the last time I'm going to explain this. You know I love you, Hope. I couldn't wait to get away from those other jerks. I just went back to my room to change my clothes and I sat down for about five minutes and I just crashed. That's all. That's the absolute truth. You know, Hope, you're not the only one who's under a strain."

I let him kiss me then. I said I believed him, and I never saw a guy look more relieved than he did. How could he have wanted to be with Grace Carnahan anyhow? She was a total fat ass. She must have weighed a hundred and thirty pounds.

Funny thing, it turned out that Brook liked the "authenticity" of my anger in the scene with the nurse. So I had to keep doing it.

And Logan was telling the truth.

About Grace, that is.

What he wasn't telling the truth about was worse, a whole lot worse.

But I didn't know anything about that then. I was just like Juliet, a big-eyed girl in love. I couldn't see anything else.

It was right after Homecoming when he first suggested it.

The Idea.

We had been out in the cabin making love during the hour between dinner and rehearsal. We pretended we were going jogging. Sometime I would be so weak from his love, I could hardly walk back to rehearsal.

The way we made love it was always like it was the first time. People say it's not always like that, that it can become routine. But the sex wasn't even the important part. It was our bodies doing what our hearts already did, like in a way we could be closer together emotionally. If we could have been inside each other's hearts, we would have been. Like wherever Logan touched me wasn't really alive until he put his hand there. He made me alive and human and real, and the world just snapped into focus when we were together. The rest of the time it was sort of shades of gray to me. If you've never done it with someone you love, I feel so sorry for you, because you can never understand this. Maybe it's only that way for people who are totally sensitive in the first place. Anyway, it was one of those special nights when he showed me the spot off the running path where the bend went up and around a little hill. He spread out a blanket, the same blanket they found me on, and we sat down and held each other. It was a pretty cool night, so we didn't do it again (Logan actually thought it was kind of gross to do it more than once). And then he asked me, "What would you say your parents think you're worth?"

VII

'M NOT A complete fool.

I know sometimes women don't see the signs, and some women don't even want to. But he was my first love and my only love. I will never love anyone like that again. So it wouldn't even have occurred to me to not trust him. To me, that's what love means. Total and complete trust. I'll never trust anyone again like I trusted Logan. Never. I'll never allow it. I never trusted my parents that much. And I never had a real friend until him. He was my soulmate.

Until The Idea took over.

When we were together, really together, if you know what I mean, he would be saying, "It would be so easy, Hope. We could get one of those voice-disguising things and use a disposable cell phone. And after the drop, I'll just be the one who finds you. You wouldn't be hurt. You know I wouldn't harm a hair on your head. But if we had, like, twenty thousand dollars stashed away, it would be so much easier. Maybe we could go off together, plus go to Hawaii, too, or something. Wouldn't you like that? You and me on a beach in Maui?" I would put my hand over his lips, but he'd just keep on. "They've got the money, honey. They're not going to miss it. And you can say it was that guy in the truck you made up the first night we were together. Remember that night? Remember when we decided that we were the ones for each other, and no one else?"

I did remember, and I went as soft as a down pillow beneath him. I couldn't resist him any more than a poor little bird can resist a beautiful cobra. I was about as able to resist as Jell-O when it came to Logan. So I agreed, yeah, we could talk more about it.

And then all he did was talk about it! I could put duct tape around my hands and then step through my arms so that it would look like someone had tied me up from behind. He would put a gag on me carefully so I could breathe easily. It was freaky, but it was exciting, too. I started to get into it a little, especially after he said how much publicity there would be after I was found safe!

Why was I such a fool?

I mean, yeah, it was logical to worry about money;

but it was a whole year before we were going to run away. There might be a summer stock theater job for me, and I would get my birthday and Christmas money, and he still got a check from his parents and from his agent every month. Now, although it disgusts me to think about it, I would bet that Alyssa Lyn talked him into it, because she was from a poor background, really white trash—I don't mean that in a bad way—she was always envious of the girls who had designer shoes. I'll bet she conned him into it by doing some disgusting sex thing. She knew my parents were pretty well off, so she tricked Logan into taking advantage of them and me. I was willing to take advantage of them too; but that's different. You don't rook your parents out of a bunch of money so another girl can have it!

It was for our dream. *Our* dream! I was desperate enough to believe in anything that would make our dream come true.

And at first I thought The Idea would just be a passing thought—kind of like one of those crazy ideas people have and then they move on. Like, wouldn't it be great if we found a lottery ticket someone dropped? Or if you found someone's Rolex watch and you could turn it in for the reward. But it wasn't, not for Logan.

You know, I shouldn't have been so blind. I had seen all the movies. From the old movies my mother insisted

I watch "for technique," like *A Place in the Sun* to *Closer* and stuff. A guy gets a woman to totally and completely trust him. She gives him her body and her heart. And then he just trashes her because he wants to move on to the next stop on the bus, as my mother used to say. Guys will do it with anyone. I'd even seen the Ben Stiller movie *Miss Fortune* that Logan was in, which is where he probably got the details for The Idea. I just totally didn't put him in a class with other males. Logan was different. I'm not even sure that he wasn't a virgin, too, the first time.

God! How could he? How could he break something that was so totally perfect and smash it and step on it and walk right over it like he didn't see it? I know the answer. Alyssa Lyn. What a total whore! The intruder was right there under my nose, next to me. Look back at my journal heading. Me, Logan and HER!

I know why I missed the signs. Really, how could anyone who had *me* want another girl? Maybe he just wanted some time to fool around because we *were* practically engaged. Maybe if he had told me, I might have forgiven him. Didn't he know that? Didn't he know he could count on my love?

It makes me insane to think about it now, how he led me on. It makes me feel like a pearl coated in slime from a swamp and rolled in dirt. Now, when I'm not crying over him, I want to scream at Logan, scream and punch him until his perfect nose breaks into mush under my hand and blood shoots out. "'Wert thou as young as I . . . Doting like me . . . then mightest thou tear thy hair, And fall upon the ground, as I do now. . . .'"

I know every line of that play. Even his.

And that one describes how I felt.

At first, when I knew he was hanging out with her, not dating but hanging out with her and her friends, more and more, I did little things to tell him I still cared and I understood. I sent him notes and sealed them with a lipstick kiss. Then, after Alyssa Lyn thought she had him, it was so awful. But I *still* didn't break trust with Logan and come out and demand that he let us be seen together. Not even when she started wearing black and white, my colors, in a totally obvious imitation. And she had the nerve to drop little hints that she thought I was doing up my hair in a messy ponytail and letting little wisps hang down because *she* did it. I heard her tell Monica that I "looked up to her." What BS! Girls are just utterly ruthless. Guys may be stupid, but girls will do anything to get what they want.

I had to do something. More than the notes. Maybe he thought I didn't care as much, because I went along with pretending we weren't together. I was just too good an actor.

I started getting a little desperate. Logan had to know

that he was still my guy! I started making little lists in my room. If he wasn't mine, why did we create The Plan and The Idea? Why did he still kiss my neck and run his hands down my shoulders in rehearsals? He didn't have to do that. Frankly, in most productions of *Romeo and Juliet*, they're panting and talking but you don't see much real physical stuff. Why did he still sit at the table behind me at lunch, at least twice a week, so my back was almost touching his? Why did he do all these things in public? Not to mention that we were making love practically every day in secret? The list that said Logan still adored me was far longer than the list that said he didn't.

I thought of mittens. Mittens are cozy and loving and they come from someone's hands and they're a sign of caring.

I had my grandma knit them. She said she couldn't do it in a week because of her arthritis, but I said it was *so* important, so she did. I dropped them off in his locker backstage in a bag I decorated with star stickers. I didn't leave a note. He didn't say anything directly, but I saw him wearing them after he came back from sledding with a bunch of people. That was just more proof. He knew exactly who those mittens were from. He even waved at me when I passed by him, going to get, like, my fourth cup of coffee of the night, and made like one of the mittens was a little puppet talking. *Hi, Hope.* I cannot tell you what that meant to me. I started practically dancing in front of the coffee vending machine. And I was totally sure he would come for me before curfew. But at dinner Alyssa Lyn was all over him like a python. How could he get away?

It was, like, two weeks before opening night.

We hadn't been together in, like . . . three days.

Maybe it was more.

I was losing track of time.

Exams were coming up, and I hadn't studied for anything.

Then there was this one Friday when I almost snapped.

A bunch of seniors were in the cafeteria having coffee. I made an excuse to pass through there on the way to my math prep (I had to have tutoring because this anxiety over Logan and the show and The Idea had messed me up so much). And Logan stood up and waved and said, "'For Juliet's sake, for her sake, rise and stand. . . .'" Alyssa Lyn was with him, sitting in the cafeteria, with her special big mug that said "Diva" on it. She sort of snarled at me and pulled him back down.

"For the real Juliet's sake, don't be a jerk," she growled at him. He held her hand. But he rolled his eyes at me.

I decided right then he could screw his big Idea.

I was going to tell him to stuff it. I was going to tell him, yes, I'd still marry him, but I wasn't going to fake being kidnapped so he could screw my parents out of money. Let him screw his own parents out of money. I was going to say that they could give him some of his earnings from his trust fund—money he'd earned from his TV guest spots and his little part in the movie—and we could use that.

But what if he broke up with me? What if he said, Fine, I'm not going through with The Plan then?

I thought about that for about five minutes and then I threw up my whole dinner.

So, I left a totally different message on his cell phone. Reverse psychology.

I said I was so excited about The Idea and could he please call me so we could figure out the details because he said it had to happen before the show—so I could come back like a little hero after having been abducted by this mysterious stranger no one would ever find. He didn't call me back. But I knew that there would be a week of school shows—shows we did for the high schools and middle schools in the area—and Brook had told him to rehearse with me before the school shows *and* after. The first school show was coming up on Wednesday. So I knew I would see him Monday. Tuesday at the latest. And alone. I would insist that we rehearse alone!

Plus, I didn't always leave the phone on, because I wasn't technically supposed to have one.

There was one missed call and, of course, it was probably him. Although now, I'm not sure. When I tell Em about that one missed call, she just shakes her head and looks sadly out of the window. I know she doesn't believe Logan ever really loved me. I don't know if I want her to believe it or if I want her to hate him as much as I hate him. Except when I love him.

He didn't call on Monday.

On Tuesday morning I stopped by his table at breakfast and said, "I'm nervous. I have to run lines. Brook said." Alyssa Lyn let out this big, fat sigh and mumbled something about high-maintenance little girls. "Logan," I repeated. "Brook said."

Logan didn't look up, but he said in a really sweet, secret way, "Fine. Can I finish eating first?"

Alyssa Lyn said, "I can help you guys."

I said, really sweetly, "No, Alyssa Lyn, you're so good. You make me tense." She just shook her hair back. The same way I do, by the way!

I forgot to tell about the ring! I brought the ring with me. Duh! That's one more proof! Would he have taken the ring if he didn't love me as much as I loved him?

It was my brother's, the ring my grandfather Shay had given Carter before he died, and it had a real ruby in it. It was old and pure gold and cut with all these curlicues and junk that made up his initials, C.S.S.— Carter Sebastian Shay—which were partly Carter's initials, too, because he was named Carter Sebastian Romano. The initials looked like a design of a dragon, because my grandfather had been an importer from Hong Kong. He imported cloth and junk. I called Carter on Monday about six in the morning and said that it looked old and I needed it for a prop. There was nowhere else I could get a man's ring that fast, even from eBay, not that my parents wouldn't kill me for buying an expensive ring on eBay. There wasn't a jewelry store for fifty miles that sold anything but rings that expanded and contracted, the kind tourists buy.

But Carter was a total chuff. He just calmly said, "Look, Detta. I'm sorry, but I can't do that." He just spoke right up like he was talking to anyone!

I said, "It's Hope, you fruit. Don't call me Detta. And you have to. You don't have any choice, you little crap. I said I need it."

"Hope, then," Carter had said. "Can't you wait until we come up to see your show? This was Grandpa's. It's all I have of his. If somebody loses it, Mom is going to freak and so am I."

"Nobody will lose it," I said. "And if you tell Mom, I'll kill you." He knew I meant it. I would make him suffer. "Carter, if you don't do this one thing for me, I'll never speak to you again. Never in my life. I mean it. All I ask you is one little thing. What have I ever asked you to do?"

"Nothing," he said. "You never even said this much to me in your whole life."

"So do you think maybe it's important to me if I'm calling you up and begging you?" I practically sneered at him. What was the big deal? He never wore it. He was only thirteen years old. I told him the combination of the safe my father had under his desk—it was the zip code of our street—and he got it out and FedExed it to me in a padded envelope. When he called me whining about it, I told him that if anybody lost it, I would sell my ear-rings, which were made from stones from Grandpa Shay's wedding band, and replace it. He kept on about how it wouldn't be the same, it wouldn't have any feel-ings attached to it, so I hung up on him. Jesus, it was like everything in the world was conspiring to drive me totally crazy! And you never act crazy or desperate around a guy! You always keep them a little at a distance. You have to pretend you don't care as much as you do, even after you confess your love. You have to pretend you could turn it on and off.

But I couldn't do it anymore. I was too far gone.

When Logan showed up where I told him to come (the piano rehearsal room because it was empty that morning; I checked the schedule and no one was using it), I ran to him and hugged him. It was such a relief after pretending for so long. He was probably almost a foot taller than I am. Well, not really. He's only about five-ten. But it felt like that. I held onto him and I said, "Logan, Logan. I can't stand it anymore. I can't go on."

He held me back by the shoulders and said, with this warm gleam in his eyes that made my mouth water like it does when you're trying not to throw up, "You're just nervous. Concentrate on being Juliet right now. Let's be pros now, Hope. Tomorrow will be a big night for you."

I held up my hand, as if I were swearing in court. "'The play's the thing,'" I said. I tried so hard to act cool and professional, but just the way he smelled reminded me of so many things. A million scenes were flashing through my head like a dream movie. Logan and me on the floor of the cabin. Logan and me on a mountaintop, at sunrise. Logan and me on a beach. But we'd never been on a mountaintop, or a beach. It was all whipping around in my mind so that I couldn't even remember where I was.

Logan patted me on the shoulder, and said, "Hope. You're a million miles away." The he added, joking, "'I profane thee with my unworthiest hand. . . .'"

"'O then, dear saint, let lips do what hands do. . . .'"

"Hope," Logan said, "you're a complete doll. And if you were two years older—"

"What," I said, "my age matters now. Since when? What are you talking about?" It was a good thing the room was soundproof because I was screaming. I was screaming and ready to start crying.

"It should matter to you," he said. "If your parents knew how you act around me—"

"Forget about my parents," I said, and I gave the ring to him, and I said, "This is for luck. 'This ring to my true knight.'"

Logan said, "Toots, I can't accept this." He turned it over in his hands. "It has someone's initials in it!"

I said, "I got it on eBay. It's totally fine. It's for luck. I paid ten bucks for it. It's vintage. And it's just a loan. For the show." Guys never spot a lie like that. Plus, they have no idea what clothes cost. They think you can get a really nice pair of jeans for twenty bucks. Their mothers keep buying them clothes until they're, like, old enough to get married. I could never have bought something that was real gold for ten dollars. It was probably worth a couple of thousand bucks or something. Or at least a hundred.

"It's beautiful," he said. The way his face got all dreamy kind of made me forget how much Carter loved the ring, how he kept a special polishing cloth for it and everything. I thought then, maybe I would let Logan keep it, not give it back to Carter at all. Hey, I thought, we have three other grandparents. One of them was bound to die someday and leave him something just as nice. "Well, then, I thank you, my most fair lady," Logan said, making a big bow to me. "Now. You promised we could get to work." He slipped on the ring. It fit just perfectly. "I have the run-through and sound check tonight, and about four thousands things to do, plus studying, before the first school show."

I wanted to pout, but didn't. It wouldn't be smart or professional.

"I'm busy too," I said. You always tell a guy you're busy. All I wanted to do was feel his arms around me.

But all Logan did was stroke my hair and say, "I personally think you look the part more than Alyssa Lyn. I always saw Juliet as dark."

"Thank you," I said. I hugged him again, and I know— I've told Em this—he hugged me back. He couldn't help it. "Oh, thank you. Thank you for seeing me as your Juliet. That means so much coming from you."

"Well, in a few years, you'll be able to do this role blindfolded, Hope. You're a good little actor. But now we need to get down to work—"

"Can we just talk for a minute first?" I asked him.

"Let's run through whatever scene makes you the most nervous."

"But we need to talk about The Idea," I said. "I'm ready and everything."

"If you're ready, what do we have to talk about?" Logan asked. He looked around him like he was checking the doors to see if anyone was coming. I realized then how totally secretive we still had to be. There were security cameras everywhere on the campus. He was so much smarter. And I knew then that his saying I was "ready" meant that the time for The Idea had come. I had to brace myself. It was going to have to be after the school show at Black Sparrow Lake High the following night. He didn't have to say the exact words. That was the way we were together. But I had to make sure.

"Should we do this tonight or tomorrow night?" I asked.

Logan looked at me oddly. I guess he thought I was an idiot because I didn't understand. After all, we were practically one person. "Hope, it's now or never. Come on, what do you want to run through?" He looked at his watch. The ring sparkled on his strong hand, with the ruby like a little heart deep inside it. He turned it around. "Are you sure you want to let me use this?"

I told him of course I was sure and that I wanted to run through the balcony scene. It's the hardest scene in the play to do, though anyone would think it's the easiest.

People have it memorized—even in regular, retard high school, some teachers make kids memorize it. It's familiar, so you have to do something to keep it new.

But now I was thinking about all the things we needed for The Idea, so I could hardly concentrate on doing what I loved doing most. I loved watching Logan pretend to walk away, and then act as if he heard a sound and say, almost like he was shocked and goofing off, "'But, soft! What light through yonder window breaks?'"

We rehearsed for an hour and a half.

Then I went to my room to sleep with tea bags on my eyes.

I used to be able to fall asleep instantly. I'd trained myself to do that so I could take an afternoon nap before a performance, because it totally clears out your mind. You're an empty vase, with the character filling you up from your subconscious. And if you sleep right before, you look all fresh when you wake up, not all liney and puffy like my mother does. The tea bags make your eyes sparkle, too, and darken your lashes naturally. You always sleep on your back.

But I couldn't sleep. I was too tense. I just lay there for a while and tried to do yoga breathing. Then I got up, and I packed my makeup bag because I wouldn't use their stuff (I have my own stage makeup for extra-sensitive skin) and checked that I had all my packets of concentrated liquid and my two layers of pants stuffed under the bed with the tape and junk. I had to take a taxi down the road to the shopping center during study hour before dinner and get a few extra things.

It turned out that I really didn't. I already had the stuff. I was so nervous that I'd forgotten that I got it when they took us to shop the Saturday before. Well! It had been a weird month. The weirdest month of my life. Falling in love. Getting a starring role. Planning to run away with the man you didn't even know you were dreaming of meeting until you met him. Faking a kidnapping because you were a good enough actor to pull off something like that. Buying your freedom. It was a lot for a fifteen-year-old to take in.

That night Brook drove me and Logan to the high school in his car, while the other cast members went in the two green school vans. Just before we got out of the car, he handed me the Black Sparrow Lake paper with an interview they had done with me, like, a week before, about playing Juliet when I was the real age of Juliet.

"It's an amazing experience," I said. "I really know how it feels to be totally in love and have it be totally hopeless and have the world not understand. Nobody understood how Juliet could want to die if she couldn't be with Romeo. They would have said, 'You're rich and beautiful. Think of the future. This guy is getting banished.' But she didn't want to live without him. Obviously I wouldn't do that. But I get it."

It was so weird that I had forgotten even talking to the reporter.

And he was the theater critic. He talked about how poised I was for my age and what a good sense of humor I had, how "natural" I was and yet so "innocent." It was on page five of the section, though, with only my freshman-year head shot; but Brook was really impressed. He said, "Now you live up to that, Hope." I promised I would, and Brook kissed me on the forehead.

You cannot imagine the reception we got.

Four curtain calls. Four! Brook was practically hysterical. He said to me and Logan, "You made those kids *get* Shakespeare!"

Despite everything I had been through, and even though I knew what I was going to do later that night, I was a total pro. I put the emotions aside. My training took over and I *fell into* Juliet. My tears were real. I never stumbled over a single line. Even stupid high school kids in the bleachers were crying and sighing.

My parents were crying, and even Carter was clapping his head off. Logan picked me up like I was a little doll and spun me around during the second curtain call.

My mother handed him some white roses and he took one and gave it to me; and I gave him one of my peach roses—fifteen, one for every year of my life. The school gave me another bouquet, too. I was practically staggering under flowers.

That was the picture they ran on the front page of the papers Saturday. The front page of papers as far away as Detroit and Madison and Chicago and Minneapolis.

The picture was like, five by seven inches.

But the story was not about the play. It was about my disappearance.

VIII

THERE'S LOGAN. And there's me. And there are my parents, back again. Up there at the top of my page.

Logan shouldn't actually be there.

The three of us, alone against the world.

That's how I saw it. But now, basically, they've ditched me.

I suppose it should be just one little I. Me, alone against the world.

But that doesn't go with my journal headings. I like things neat.

I went from being a star—okay, it was just in front of a high-school audience, but it would have been in front of big-time agents and scouts from Hollywood and everything—to being a suspected criminal literally overnight. It didn't happen the way Logan said it would.

Maybe he chickened out. Maybe Alyssa Lyn talked him out of saving me. Maybe he wanted to make a fool of me because secretly he knew that I outclassed him as an actor.

And it makes want to pull out my hair that I did it myself. I shot my own balloon out of the sky. But only because Logan told me to. I was afraid, but I had to believe him. It was like stories in that book I read about Princess Diana. I was a lamb to the slaughter. She said that. I know how she must have felt—like, beautiful, and everyone thinking you must be so happy, but totally sad and confused. I had so many notes with so many maps and so many directions for The Idea, they were all getting jumbled in my head. And I didn't keep them! There were so many of them that they were like a book! When the police asked me later on to show them the notes Logan gave me, I started to laugh. I told them that they had to be kidding. Like I could keep those notes, any more than I could keep his love letters? I burned the love letters and I burned the notes, right after he gave them to me, in a rice bowl I had put in my purse once when we were at Sumo Sushi in New York. It was a bowl where I normally kept my earrings. They wanted to see the bowl to check for ashes.

What did they think, that I didn't wash it?

There were no ashes in that bowl.

I couldn't believe how stupid and suspicious they

were, right from the beginning. They always blame the victim. The police were no different from anyone else involved. I have a very good memory, I told the police— when they came to do the so-called investigation. I should have, after, like, eight years of memorizing lines. It was all in my head. And I wanted to tell them the truth. But . . . the police! It was so terrifying! And my head, which was normally so clear, was filled with arguing voices and arguing thoughts. Should I? Shouldn't I? If I did, would Logan still love me? Or would he turn to Alyssa-the-Bitch? He would never let me go through this alone. Or would he? He wouldn't abandon me!

On top of everything, I got an academic probation slip for the second quarter where I had gone from As to Cs because of all the stress I was under, good and bad. I'd given up everything for Logan, and after the performance, he got weird, staying away from me.

The thing was, after the show, after the flowers, I went from being a girl to being an outlaw, a person completely dedicated to one person and to our dream. Like Van Gogh. Or Gandhi. Outside society's rules, which were dumb anyhow.

This is how it all happened. As best as I can remember.

It took me a while to get back to my room that night of the first performance. My parents insisted on taking me out to dinner. I wanted to go to the first cast party with all the other kids, but my mother said I should celebrate with family and make an early night of it. "With a debut like that, you have to stay focused, Hope. You don't know who's going to read that interview and come to the next show. My God, people in New York could read it! Being an understudy in a production like this is no small thing, Hope." I just stared her down. Calling me an understudy after that debut? And getting all excited about a little town's newspaper story. The Black Sparrow Lake newspaper wasn't exactly *USA Today*, although *USA Today* would try to interview me later. I didn't talk to them.

My mother said I could go to the *closing* night party, when it wouldn't matter how I looked for the next show, in case I needed to be Juliet. I didn't know what the hell she was talking about.

And so, after I finally got rid of my parents, I carefully put just the smallest sliver of cardboard in the glass doors of the dorm, just like I had so many times before, so the alarm wouldn't go off when I opened the door.

And then I waited for Logan. I thought that he'd come and get me by one a.m. at the latest. But then I remembered he would be at the cast party, and it probably lasted until all hours. I could see the lights on in the lodge. Then the lights went out.

Everybody probably went to the shack afterward, I thought. So, about one thirty or so, I put on my hiking boots and my parka. I went up the jogging path and then turned off into the woods toward the shack. And there they were, all the seniors, with a big keg. All I had to do was to take one picture with my cell phone and they'd all be expelled. Logan and Alyssa Lyn were in the middle of the floor, grinding away to some stupid ChanTwos song they had on a boom box. Then, all of a sudden, one of them whispered, "Can it! I hear something!"

"Hit the lanterns! No, all of them!"

They did, and I accidentally dropped my flashlight and ran. That was when I first found *my* little ravine, because I dived right into it when I heard the door bang open.

"Flashlight. See over there!" somebody said.

"Better split."

"Sure it's not Logan's little shadow? Tinkerbell?"

A voice I sort of recognized said, "Rose, you should stop encouraging her. You bring it on yourself. She probably thinks you want her."

And Logan said, "I don't come on to her or anything. She's a good kid."

"You don't have to! She's totally like a little puppy dog, following you around with her tongue out!" the guy said. "Ready for action!"

Everybody laughed.

A girl's panicky voice broke in then, "It's almost two in the morning! If we get caught out here . . ."

Alyssa Lyn, almost crying, said, "I don't want to get kicked out of the show! I don't want to get kicked out of school!"

So they all left.

They took the flashlight, and it was so dark I couldn't see my hand in front of my face. But I managed to follow close enough behind them that I could see the light bobbing along.

I went back to my room and lay there on the bed. I wished I could just sleep until I was old, like, twenty-one.

I just lay there. I felt like I could hear my life cracking and creaking and breaking like the limbs of an old tree in a high wind. I wanted to call Logan and scream, "I saw you practically screwing her with your clothes on! What about me? What about The Plan? What about The Idea?"

I thought, The hell with Logan Rose.

But the more I thought about him with her, the more I knew I had to go through with it because he was weak, and she would get him away from me. And so I got up and started to get dressed. First my black long underwear, then my black jogging pants and matching hoodie, and then finally my gloves and silk ski mask turned up like a hat. I packed my little pack with a few granola bars, some water bottles, condensed moisture packets, a few of those things you crack open to warm your hands at football games, and other stuff I would need. I took my cell, too. At least I could use it to surf the Net when I was bored. There was going to be a lot of dead time for me. I wished I had my flashlight. I carefully opened the dorm door and the alarm did not go off. I started to jog in the dark, hoping I wouldn't twist my ankle.

As I warmed up, I thought about the fact that The Idea wasn't totally original. In fact, it was sort of just like the plot of *Miss Fortune*, the movie with Ben Stiller where Logan had two lines. Right down to the disposable cell phone, and using one of those kids' Darth Vader voice-changing masks, except the guy was going to ask for a million dollars instead of twenty thousand. If my parents didn't tell the police and left the money in regular cash where he said to leave it, "the kidnapper" would tell them where to find me. But if they told the police, they would never find me. I would be dead from natural causes in a few days unless they did what he said, because he would just leave me where I was.

Logan could just walk away and no one would ever know.

But he had to be planning to do what we had always said—act like he was the hero who saved my life, and my parents would still love him after we ran away.

In the movie, the guy played by Ben Stiller is this rich guy whose parents have cut him off because he's, like, thirty, and he's flunked out of college, like, five times. The girl he talks into The Idea does just what he tells her to, and ties him up. But the next morning they dig up the whole forest where he's tied to a tree for a condominium development, and he ends up in a bucket machine or something. The girl takes off with the money. The last thing you see is her driving this big red pickup truck and picking up . . . Logan (or the character he played).

He says to her, "Hey, good looking? Are you headed where I'm going?"

She says, "Has it got palm trees and tequila?"

He says, "It does now!"

And they take off, burning rubber, in Ben Stiller's jazzed-up truck.

I finally found the place where Logan had said I should wait. The little short evergreens and bushes would hide me and keep me warm. The jogging path went on for miles, but Logan and I usually only did a circuit, a mile and a half out and a mile and a half back. We only went farther, out to the hunter's cabin, for . . . you know what. But after I found the place, I went out to the cabin. It was still warm in there from the after-party party. I went in and lay on the floor, and the smell of beer and cigarettes made me nauseated. I looked in the little broom closet and got out our special sleeping bag.

I thought about Logan. About our love and how

suspicious I was. And how strange this thing was that he'd asked me to do. I want to be clear right now. I didn't know *exactly* for sure why he wanted me to do it. He said it was for the money, for The Plan. But maybe he really wanted the attention to help launch our careers. It would be in newspapers all over the country, with pictures of him and me. All publicity is good, I thought. I thought that would be okay.

Romeo Rescues Juliet.

Right.

I woke up in the cabin. I was still pretty warm in the sleeping bag, but I could tell it had gotten colder.

I didn't want to put the tape around my hands until the last possible minute.

But Logan said I had to do it a little sooner so it would look authentic when he found me the next day. The tape would have to be on six or eight hours before the rescue at least. Overnight, if I could stand it. Otherwise, it would look phony. It had to look like I'd actually been kidnapped and missing for four days. He wouldn't let me get too bad off. After all, I was his love, "the sweetest flower of all the field." It would just be more dramatic when I *somehow managed to take the stage again the next weekend* for the Saturday night performance. People would be wowed. It would be a national story.

The whole thing had gone according to the way it was supposed to this far. Just before my mother kissed me good night after dinner, I said I'd seen that creepy guy again. I said I thought it was the guy who worked at the shopping center restaurant, Chatters, the Mexican guy. He was the only guy I knew by sight who was in his twenties. She freaked and said she was going to tell the administration the next day. And I said no, I didn't want Mr. Emerson to get upset. He would flip out.

That shut her up.

She wouldn't have cared if Jeffrey Dahmer was stalking me if it was going to bother *Brook Emerson*.

Finally, after a whole day of doing nothing but jogging to keep warm and then sleeping, I got ready to tie myself up. I went to the place and I laid down outside and taped my hands in front of my body.

And Logan didn't come.

When he didn't come the first night, I did have the thought that maybe he'd dumped me. Then I pushed it away. He knew I had food and a warm place to go. He probably couldn't get away from his parents. That's all. But the bad thoughts kept creeping back.

He really had dumped me!

The Idea wasn't about me.

He was really going to run away with Alyssa Lyn Davore!

With my parents' money.

He was planning to let me die out there. Not like I was stupid enough to let that happen. But I could have been that stupid. I could have killed myself.

My parents probably already knew about it too. The police already probably knew about it. No, they wouldn't know until morning.

I got up and ripped off the tape, went back into the cabin, wrapped myself in the sleeping bag, and checked the weather on my cell. No snow in the forecast, just cold, and not below freezing. I fell asleep. I woke up when I heard someone coming, laughing, crunching along. It had to be people coming to the cabin to be alone, the way Logan and I had. I made a howling noise—I don't know why, but I couldn't think of what else to do—and I heard a scream and footsteps crashing away. It was so cold I curled up in a ball with the sleeping bag over my head.

Now, I would have gone back to my dorm right then except a part of me still wanted to believe that Logan, *my* Logan, would come to me.

But there was another part of me thinking something else, and that part was growing bigger.

It was like a red flower in my chest, growing bigger and brighter. I wanted to make him pay.

Pay for snuggling with Alyssa Lyn in the lounge. Pay

for grinding with her at the secret party. Pay for . . . using me and leaving me in the cold. Alone. I was so incredibly furious that I decided to let him think that I was gone, really gone, not for pretend.

So when the sun came up, I took my tape and my junk but I didn't go to the place where I was supposed to be found. Instead, I went to my little gully, which was behind the hill—like, half a mile away, farther past the old hunting cabin on the circle trail. There was a little bridge over a dry creek, and I scrunched under it and put on the tape. Now, it wasn't exactly at the bottom of the ocean! Anyone looking along that bend away from the circular jogging path could have seen me, but they'd have to be looking and not be total idiots.

I lay down there, under the bridge, sucking on a moisture packet. If anyone got anywhere near me, I figured I could pretend I was passed out. But though I heard shouts and sirens, nobody came remotely close by. I went back into the cabin that night. It was cold; I made a little fire in the oven with some paper and dry branches I broke off a tree. It was smoky, but it was warm. I got into my down bag and went to sleep.

The next morning I was bored out of my mind. I wanted to play games on my cell, but I needed to save the battery to check on the weather. When I tried to do that, I saw that there was a story in the Black Sparrow

Lake paper Friday night and that Saturday morning in the Detroit paper, about this huge manhunt for the missing "young actress" from Starwood.

Me!

I decided I would go back out to my special place and put in the gag and bind myself up for real.

Logan must have been out looking in the place we originally decided on and not been able to find me! Now he was sorry. Now he would remember everything we meant to each other and stop being such an asshole. He must have practically had a seizure from fear. He must have started praying, saying to God he would do anything if I was just safe. I pulled down my silk ski mask over my face and went running to warm up before going to lie down. I passed a guy running in the opposite direction, but he was a real hot dog going about ten miles an hour, and he didn't even look at me.

I ran straight out toward the edge of the woods, where I'd never been, and straight back.

Then, back at the cabin, I put my hands on the stove where it was still warm from the little fire I'd made in the dark. It would be cool before anyone came looking. I didn't think until later that anyone might have seen the smoke. I checked the Internet again. I was amazed that my cell phone worked, until I realized that I was actually only a few hundred yards from the administration building. It just *felt* remote, because of the woods. Friday night, it had said in the Black Sparrow Lake newspaper that Alyssa Lyn Davore had dedicated her performance the night before to me. She came out after the curtain and said, "If anyone here knows anything about where Hope is, please help us. Hope is one of us. If I ever did anything to hurt her, I'm so sorry. We just want her to be safe."

Stinking bitch.

It had warmed up so much I was actually sweating from my run. I could hear all kinds of cars, and people shouting, so I thought I should go outside and get in position. But there was another article, and I had to read it.

Volunteers were coming from as far away as Madison and Chicago!

After that, I knew I was ready to really take the risk and be out overnight. After all, it said they were already doing flyovers with helicopters and, even though the woods were dense, those things probably had heat-sensing units in them. With my luck, they would sense a dead deer or two people screwing. Oh, well. They had to find me somehow.

It was the biggest thing to happen in Black Sparrow Lake, ever!

Even if Logan had changed The Idea, people all over the country were still going to see *my* face when I was found! All I needed was one casting director to see my face and think I was the one. The Idea might have been stupid, but nobody was going to be paying attention to little Starwood's production of *Romeo and Juliet*. They were going to be searching for me! I thought of all the girls who had ignored me, who were now standing outside the dorm and singing and holding candles.

And if they were cold standing out there, it served them right.

Reading about your own kidnapping is like going to your own funeral. I told Em that, and she wrote back that she always thought angels could look down at their own funerals, which was sort of random. But I knew what she meant.

Anyhow, there was no way that even morons could have failed to find me that day. The news stories all said the searchers were going out in wider and wider circles. So I had to make it look real, or I would be the one who got in trouble.

I went to lie down in the little gully and I used the tape to tie up my hands yet again. I filled up with water before I did it, and I made sure the gag was a clean wet handkerchief, so I could suck on it if I got thirsty, which I would.

Then came the cold night. No one had predicted that it would get down to ten degrees. No one had said it would even get below freezing.

It was the most terrifying thing that ever happened to me. Probably it was the most terrifying thing that ever happened to anyone.

I could hear the searchers tromping right past me. And I was so sure that they would find me right away that when I heard them going away, I got hysterical. I made noises, but they were making so much noise themselves they couldn't have heard me if I had been playing the tuba! I cried so hard that the lashes on my eyes froze. It was even too cold to snow, which was good I guess, because at least I didn't get wet. I had tied myself up so well, I couldn't get loose. I kept falling asleep and had to wake myself up. I knew if I didn't, one of those times I would fall asleep and never wake up. Carter would never see me again. My parents would be scarred for life! But I fell asleep anyway.

It got warmer during the morning. After a while I stopped shaking. But I couldn't stop crying.

I realized that drinking all that water was a big miscalculation.

I had peed myself and I was in total agony, itching and burning. The gag was making my mouth bleed at the corners. I didn't know anything about gags! I didn't know they could be tied too tight. I couldn't even bite down on the tape on my wrist because this last time I had taped my ankles and then my hands, and then jumped through my arms so that they were behind me. There was no way I could jump back. So I couldn't even get to my knees.

I semi-knew I was going to die on the fourth night.

I sort of half wanted to die, or at least get really sick.

People had to feel *something* when they found me after all I had been through. No one understood, even afterward, that I was the one who did the suffering. How could they not feel sorry for someone who'd been abandoned in a ditch all night, all because she listened to someone older who was supposed to love her? They should have been saying I was the bravest girl they'd ever met. I comforted myself for a while with picturing the spread in *People* magazine, with some police officer standing next to the little bridge, an arrow pointing to the place "where Hope was left." I practiced what I would say: "I knew that I was going to live. I had to live. People can do wrong to you, but you have to listen to that little voice inside you that says you're meant to do something in this world, no matter who tries to throw you off track."

Finally I told myself, Hope, you're a survivor. You've survived starving yourself and seventeen performances of *Annie*, even when you had to go on with the flu. You survived all those rejections when you auditioned that summer.

I thought about Alyssa Lyn. I knew some people are evil. But I never knew a really evil person. She was just evil. Like in the play: "Was ever book containing such vile matter So fairly bound?" That's Alyssa Lyn. Alyssa Lyn is pretty. Some people would say she's beautiful. And she is totally experienced. Much more than me. She must have slept with half the guys at Starwood. I mean, totally perverted. I was innocent, except for Logan, and he loved me. She knew that. She could never have that same quality of innocence I had, no matter how much like Alice in Wonderland she looked. Why do guys get taken in by these girls? Like, Alyssa Lyn might someday be a B movie actor or even a model for a chain department store. But she is not the real thing, as an actor or as a person. Why don't men see that? Why don't they see inside women the way we see inside them?

And dedicating her performance to me, in the role she stole.

What a complete pig. What a phony.

And what about Logan?

Was he really as bad as she was? I knew if I could just talk to him, just once, he would see that what he did was more than cheating on me. He would get it. I was too good a judge of character to fall for a phony. I might have been young, but I had known a lot of people. A *lot* of people. And I could spot phonies right away. I could tell people were lying even when they didn't know it themselves. I could always spot the people making excuses for why they were fat or why they didn't get a role. They were all afraid. So they didn't even try. They couldn't let their real selves show. It was uncomfortable for them to be around someone who did, like I did.

I have to be rational about it now, even though it still hurts.

My pride is hurt.

Not the real me. The real me knows the truth.

It's totally possible that on some level, Logan was threatened by me. Yes, we would have been perfect together, but eventually, I would have gone farther than he did. I see it all so clearly now. He was the real loser. He lost me. He's going to have a smaller future because he won't have me.

He can never admit what he did. He'd go to jail. He's eighteen. Kidnapping is a crime you can get the death penalty for. Even so, I felt sure that eventually someone would find out the truth if I died.

Then I realized if I died, I would never be a star. I would just be a beautiful face in a newspaper.

So I reached down into the bottom of my soul and I called on all my strength and I started to fight.

I struggled against the tape, but my hands were swollen from the cold, and the tape was wrapped so tight that they were practically numb. It wasn't going to work. Finally I used my hands like a snowplow to push me out from under the bridge, even though they got all scratched up from the brush and started bleeding in a couple of places. It was nearly impossible to go on. Someone else might have given up. But I'm not someone else. There may not be much of me, but what there is never gives up.

I kicked and pushed my bottom half out of the little trench under the bridge. I pulled myself with the heels of my shoes until most of my legs would be visible—that is, if it weren't dark. I cried and I promised God that if I got rescued, I would give Carter back his ring.

And finally, they found me.

Early in the morning, a dog came up and sniffed me and started to walk away, but then the owner, this tall lady with a Sherlock Holmes hat on, came running along, yelling, "What is it, Lurcher? What is it, boy?" Like the dog was a genius. The idiot mutt had practically tripped over my feet. Then she started screaming into her radio, "Central! Alert! This is Whooping Crane. We have located the girl! I have her!"

I don't remember much about them rushing me to the hospital, the warming blankets, the ambulance, my father's face. Because of my insulating underwear, and two pairs of socks, I didn't have frostbite at all. They gave me fluids in an IV and put some ointment on my scratches. Then they let me go back to the bed and breakfast with my parents.

My parents got me my own room, though my mother insisted on sitting in the chair by my bed all night, which meant I couldn't use my cell phone.

I just wanted some food and some privacy. A cheeseburger and fries.

I got my mother, tomato soup, and an old, stale cookie.

The next morning detectives were all over me.

Could I describe the kidnapper?

I told them he knocked me out. So, uh, no? Like, I was unconscious? This was going to be easy, I thought at first.

Well, then, they asked, why didn't they find any bruises on my head?

I said, "How the hell should I know? I was knocked out." I told my mother, "Make them leave."

But she didn't. She said they wanted to find the man.

They told me that I *had* to have seen the man before he knocked me out. If he dragged me all the way from my dorm, like I said. I said he had on a ski mask. They asked if it was like the silk ski mask that I had on. They brought in a sketch artist. Finally, my parents said I needed to rest, to recuperate from the shock, that we needed some time alone.

But the police told them that they had a narrow window of opportunity to catch this guy, and all they needed was my description of what happened right then. I got so panicky that when I finally got some real food, I could only eat half of my toast and omelet, and except for the power bars and the crummy canned soup, I hadn't had anything to eat in four whole days! If I said anything, I would get Logan in trouble. I don't know why I cared! But then things got weird.

The police had searched my dorm room. They'd found the receipt for the duct tape and underwear. I told them that the tape was for sealing the windows because my room was drafty, and the longies were for running.

Then they said that a jogger had passed a young woman my size running in the woods when I was supposed to be tied up. Was that me? The clothes were the same as the clothes I was wearing. . . . Christ! How did *they* know this stuff? So fast?

So I described the guy who cleaned off the tables at Chatters. I said he was short and had a Mexican accent and had big shoulders and long hair in a ponytail.

I thought he was probably illegal anyhow.

I asked to see Logan.

They called him and they put him on the phone.

He told me he was so glad I was okay.

That was it.

He was so glad I was okay? What the hell did he mean by that? I practically begged him, "Can you come and see me right now?"

He said, "I don't think that's a good idea, Hope. Just rest and get better."

I asked him, "Is *Alyssa Lyn* going on in the show in my place?"

He said, "Your place? That doesn't even matter. Don't worry about stuff like that, Hope. Just . . . get better. Jesus, if I thought I had anything to do with this . . . Hope, you could have died out there!"

That's when I knew.

He wasn't going to admit to anything.

I later found out that they only let me talk to him in the hopes that whatever he said to me would make me admit to something. Me! Not him!

When I got off the phone, I started to cry.

My father said to the police, "Can't this wait?"

But this one detective who was really weasly looking, like the actor who always plays the killer, said, "We don't have time for a bunch of tears right now, Bernadette."

I said, "It's Hope."

He said, "It's Bernadette according to your birth certificate. Bernadette and I are going to need to talk for quite a while. You guys can go and put your feet up if you want."

My father said, "I'm a lawyer. My daughter's a minor. You can't interview her alone. You know that."

The stupid, skinny cop who looked like his gun weighed more than he did shrugged. "Does she need legal counsel?"

My father said, "I hope not. I think I'll stay right here with my child, if that's okay with you. And so will my wife."

Joe Ed Hick cop shrugged, and said, "My concern is that with you here, she'll try to cover up anything she may have had to do with this."

"You're joking," my father said. "No one would willingly go through what Hope went through."

"You'd be surprised," said Joe Ed Hick asshole. "For example, did Hope tell you at first that she had been cast in the role of Juliet, that she was going to alternate performances with Alyssa Lyn Davore?"

"Yes, and that's what would have happened if—"

"Well, she didn't, Mr. Romano. She was just Miss Davore's understudy."

He *had* to say "just," the asshole.

"Yes, but she was going to be in several of the performances. In some of the high school shows and matinees, she was going to play Juliet," my mother explained. "And she was definitely going to alternate the evening performances . . . I think. That's what she said." Even my mother didn't get it! Alyssa Lyn was really *my* understudy! That was why Logan fell in love with me. *He saw that I was the true Juliet*, not Alyssa Lyn! I just did the school show for . . . well, I didn't remember right then, and I don't remember right now, why she didn't do that school show. All I knew is that this guy had it totally messed up.

But he kept right on, and said, "No, she wasn't. She wasn't going to alternate performances. She would only have played the role during the evening performances if Alyssa got sick. . . ."

"We never—" my mother began.

"We can't imagine any of this. Lying about her role. Hope is an honest girl," my father said.

"Did you plan to do this with anyone, Hope?" Joe Ed Hick cop asked me.

I started to cry. "Mommy!" I said. "Get him out of here!"

The cop said, "I'm not saying she did anything. I'm not saying she didn't. But if she did, she's in serious trouble. Miss, you could be charged as an adult for something like this. You could be looking at jail time for fraud."

"What do you mean? What did I do?"

"I mean if you had any part in this abduction, or supposed abduction, you cost the people of Mesquakie County hundreds of thousands of dollars. Is your daddy ready to pay for it?"

"I don't know what you mean."

"Didn't you know that's what happens? You have to make restitution. You have to pay back what your little joke cost people. Do you know how many people were terrified for their own children? Or how many people took their kids out of school here? Do you know what you may have cost the volunteers who took off work?"

"I didn't ask them to take off work."

"These people cared about a little girl lost out in the woods."

"They cared so much it took them four days to find me!"

"Why aren't you more grateful, Miss Romano?"

"I am, but I don't know why you're torturing me!"

"Well, someone logged on to your Internet account while you were tied up. . . ."

"I don't know who did that. I know people. I have friends who know my password."

"Who?"

"Logan does. And other people, too! They even used to call me Tinkerbell. That's how I got the idea for my password!"

"Well, why would Logan Rose use your password to log on and check weather reports?"

"Maybe he was worried about me."

"Or maybe you did it." This guy was like an old TV

character in some show on Nick at Night. "Maybe you weren't really tied up at all. Maybe you were out there laughing at all those poor people looking for you."

"I never laughed at anyone! I was terrified I was going to die! Were you ever out alone in the cold at night like that?"

"Many times," said the weasly cop.

"Well, I'm only fifteen!"

"I know, and we're all relieved that you're safe. But there are so many things that don't make sense in your story. It's like you did this just because you were jealous of that pretty blond girl, Alyssa Lyn. . . ."

That did it. At last, I had to say it.

I sat up and yelled, "No way! It was his idea. Ask him! Just ask him! He even called it 'The Idea.' Ask Logan Rose! Ask him why I was so-called kidnapped! He planned the whole thing and he made me do it!"

And the hick said, "Well, I'll just do that."

At first Logan had at least talked to me. Then he went into "seclusion." His parents were like two big fat pigeons around their chick. But after I said what I said, and the police questioned him, his big fat brother—who's a lawyer about ten years older—came out flapping.

He said on TV, "There isn't a single shred of evidence that connects my brother to this poor girl. You don't have to take Logan's word for it. Ask anyone. She had this fixation." Blah, blah, blah. I didn't even know what "fixation" meant. Big brother said Logan took me out to have dinner the one night of tryouts as a treat and he tried to spend time with me so that he could help me learn my part, but that was it. He said I followed Logan everywhere until it drove him crazy and people noticed. He said Logan tried over and over to discourage me from thinking we could be romantically involved, but that I wouldn't listen. He said maybe his little brother had been too gentle.

Romantically involved?

What did he call that night backstage? All those nights in the cabin? The times we talked for hours about our future—bagels and a tiny little apartment and a big dog and rolling in the leaves in the park? It made my heart practically stop to hear that Logan Rose, who took my love and my virginity and my future, talked about me as if I were nothing more to him than a little puppy dog with a crush. I knew why he did it. If he admitted the truth about us, he was going to get charged with setting this all up. But it was the worst disloyalty I've ever heard of. I felt worse than I would have if my parents told me they never really wanted me—they just found me on a church step one day and took me home and fed me.

And of course, everyone else they interviewed at Starwood agreed with Logan. They all hated me, the fat-assed idiots, so they all said the same thing that Logan did: I was like this stalker. I followed Logan all over the campus and embarrassed him.

Then my own family turned on me! My brother told my parents about my grandfather's ring. My grandmother told my parents about the mittens. Everyone said I was stuck-up and thought I was a movie star and was a total pain in the ass. Jealous just like my mother said people would be all my life.

They were so jealous that they had to get rid of me. Why lie otherwise about my being the perfect Juliet? Why did the school totally, officially lie?

The only one who was true to me was Brook Emerson. He wouldn't say a bad word about me. He said I was the perfect tragic heroine, a sweet wild blossom. I read one story—it was actually a *New York Times* essay Brook wrote about the experience. He wrote,

She was the very Juliet. She had the talent for it. I seriously considered letting her go with it. But it was obvious how very, very delicate she was. She can't be held to the same standards as these big hardy Swedes. It's not easy to understand a spirit like that. It could wink out at any moment. I have a hard time, even now, believing she would do anything so wrong. I don't have a child of my own. But if I did, I would want a child as alert and sensitive, as intuitive and observant as Hope Shay was. If I'm not being too grand, I think of what Hemingway said about Fitzgerald, that his talent was so fragile it might be damaged by a touch, like the dust on a butterfly wing. Something like that must have happened to Hope.

Will Brook help me when I graduate? If he does believe in me like he wrote, I could get back on track. I could be the same Hope I was. It could happen if this place doesn't break me in half like a pencil.

The true agony is that I have to forget Logan. That means forgetting a part of myself. It's the only way I will ever feel better, but it means I have to erase the good memories, the pictures that drift across my mind.

I tell Em, "They were laughing at me the whole time. They thought they could get away with using me and blackmailing me as if I were a joke. But why?"

Em never answers.

How can she?

There just is no answer.

Honestly, it confuses me as much as it did the police. I'm not a psychologist. I don't know why people do things that they have nothing to gain from. I understand wanting attention! Especially now. But why couldn't you get attention in a good way, instead of by hurting someone else? Why do that? It totally shocks me. I was just minding my own business, studying, doing what I do best. And then Logan came along. He made the first move, in the cafeteria. I didn't intend to get involved with any boy until I was at least a junior. I knew it would be too much of a distraction. He reeled me in. I cry and cry and look up at the same moon that Logan and I looked at together, the inconstant moon, like it says in *Romeo and Juliet*. It was Logan who was inconstant. The moon is still there, gentle and pale, like the face of a sad mother. But Logan is gone. I have bad thoughts. Like, was he looking up at the moon with Alyssa Lyn at the same time? Did he . . . do it with her, too? Was all that stuff about us having to hide our love just so he could have two girls? I'll never know. They all protected Alyssa Lyn. Because she was older. Because she was part of the Starwood circle. I was the one who was the outsider, the kid who got the role all of them wanted—no matter what anyone says about it now. I was so stupid to think they would like me or understand me at Starwood. They were like sharks in a pool, and I was thrown in. I don't feel sorry for myself. But I am so sick of the way people are. They don't give you respect. They don't give you trust. That's what I hate most. You can't trust human beings any more than a pack of wild wolves. They don't have consciences. One minute they let you touch them, and the next minute they rip you apart and walk away and don't look back. You have to deal with the damage.

You don't know people until they totally betray you, I always say to Em. She gives me her sad, knowing smile.

After it was all over, after the investigation that they dragged out for weeks, probably so that the retard cops could feel important about the biggest case in their meaningless lives, they charged me with a crime.

They charged *me* with attempted fraud and obstructing a police investigation.

There wasn't even a trial. I just had to stand in front of a judge with my parents a month later. Stand there and take the sentence the judge gave me. I couldn't tell my side, my father said. This was the best I could hope for, my father said. No one was allowed to talk to me, but one photographer got to take my picture to give to all the newspapers.

But when the judge said that the crime was punishable by eighteen months in jail and a fine of ten thousand dollars, I couldn't help it. I started to moan and say, "No! No! *No!* I'm not responsible!"

But then she said, "We know that, Hope."

I thought somebody finally got it. But she only meant I was cuckoo. She said, "Calm down, Hope. There are what we call mitigating factors here. You're very young. And while this was very wrong, we don't think you are a danger to anyone in society or to yourself, and that is usually the standard for a punishment in juvenile crime. There's no reason for a trial here. In juvenile cases like these, a trial is very rare. No one was hurt, but a great deal of money and resources were wasted because of your poor choices. And so this is what I'm going to do." She gave me probation for two years because of "special circumstances." Then they made my poor father pay thousands of dollars toward the cost of the investigation.

And of course, I was expelled immediately from Starwood. I got a letter about that as soon as I got back to Miss Taylor's!

When I walked out of the Mesquakie County courthouse, all the photographers who had to stay outside went crackers and photographed me. I tried to hide under my dad's coat. I must have looked like some witch from a comic book. Big mascara stains under my eyes.

I didn't even get the chance to have *my* hair cut and styled for the cameras the way *Logan* did.

Why did this happen? Why was I blamed? It's so unfair for one innocent person to be the target of someone else's plot! I don't even know how many people were involved. Maybe it was more than Logan. Someone had to put him up to it. He couldn't have done this to me on his own.

I got Logan's new number off the Internet so at least I could say good-bye to him. That's all I wanted, really and truly. To say good-bye, my love. I wanted to be big, and forgive. Otherwise, it eats you alive, the way it has with me. I wasn't going to blame or accuse him. I had to call him from the pay phone. I waited four rings. I could hear laughing and music in the background. When Logan heard my voice, he said, "Enough of this, Hope. You poor kid." And he hung up on me. But not before I heard just a trace of the old Logan in his voice.

When I finally let the whole story out to Em, she just did one thing. She held up her arm.

And I saw the cuts on her wrists.

I knew what she was trying to suggest.

IX

I DON'T KNOW IF IT'S the end of my life or the beginning of another part of my life. But I'm writing this right before I do something so drastic it could kill me. It has to work. If it doesn't work, I'll just be gone.

That would be the worst-case scenario, like they say. I'm taking a huge risk. But I'm a risk-taker. I always have been. If I have to end my life to get them to listen, or at least make a convincing attempt at ending my life, I will. I can do it because I know how to act and people have always believed me whatever I do.

It's so sad that it's come to this, having to fake things. Having to hurt yourself to get people to see how much *you* have been hurt! I have never felt so sad in my life. So sad that my shoes are too heavy to lift. This must be what they mean by self-sacrifice.

The "X" up there, on my next-to-last journal entry,

marks the end of Hope. "X" marks the spot.

The little "I" is the Hope I was, but can't be anymore.

You know the whole story now. A life taken away, a whole bright future. This isn't just a loss to me. It's a loss to the whole world. No one will ever see me the way I would have been. I've been scarred on the inside. What will a scar on the outside matter? (Well, not a totally huge one; that would be different. I don't want to look freaky, like Em.) Right now I just look totally pale and sick. I'm glad it shows. When I look into the mirror, I see a girl whose eyes have no life and sparkle. They're like pools of muddy water. This is a tragedy, plain and simple.

I put this off. I thought Logan would come around. I thought my parents would show some sympathy.

But it has to happen.

You can only fight so long—even when you know you're right. Em knows that.

Then you have to give in. That's why she showed me her arm.

I have to give in.

Yesterday I felt so down I didn't think I could go on. The pain was unbearable, the way my mother said it is to give birth. It was like my guts were coming out. They say that people who commit suicide really want to kill someone else, and maybe for me that someone would be Logan. But all I really want—all I ever really wanted—is the chance to be heard. If I can't get heard, it would be best to go to sleep forever. I've been sleeping almost around the clock anyway. The teachers have been sending my parents reports. They told me that I was about to have a real breakthrough because they said girls usually "hit bottom" before they come up and start fighting to reclaim their lives. I have no idea what they're talking about. I'm having enough trouble with Latin verbs. Why do I have to figure out deep truths about myself, too?

When I saw those cuts on Em's arm, I knew that's how she got people to hear her.

I know she meant well. But if I did that . . . I would die for sure. I was willing to take a risk, but not if I had to count on someone else to save me. Been there, done that!

The cuts on Em's arms were . . . real. They were from a real suicide attempt that was meant to work. I know. I *saw* them. They were big, fat, ropy scars. Vertical scars. I could not imagine anyone doing that who wasn't serious.

I didn't want that much of a disfiguring thing on me. I mean, even if I died. What if they put me in a dress with three-quarter-length sleeves and had to try to disguise ugly cuts sewed up with black thread? Jesus, that's all people would see. The cuts. Not me.

So I learned how to make the other kinds of cuts from Suzette. She had them all over her arms and legs.

Some were like homemade tattoos because she actually cut herself and then drew with ink in the cuts, which I'm surprised didn't kill her from some kind of disgusting infection. She had cuts all over, in the shape of lightning bolts, roses, snakes, and just crosses. She was big on crosses.

"What's that about?" I asked her one day, last week or the week before. You do lose track of time here, because every day is the same as the day before. "They're going to lock you up someplace."

"Duh," Suzette said. "Like it would be the first, second, or tenth time."

"Why do you do it?"

She clasped both her hands together by her heart and said, "To *feel* something! That's what my shrink says. To feel the pain I won't allow myself to feel over, um, Robbie. My little brother." Suzette tucked a strand of her hair behind her ear, a gesture I've tried to do. She has amazing thick hair, but she dyes it bright red, like Bozo. "That's not really why. I do it because it's dramatic. It's cool. They put me in the infirmary and treat me like I'm a movie star."

She said she takes a whack at some part of herself about once a month. Once she took a whole handful of antidepressants. That got her a big tube up her nose and her stomach pumped. "That was not at all so cool,"

Suzette said. "I, like, want to die, but not die puking, you know?"

"You *want* to die?" I asked her.

"Oh, sure," Suzette said. "I'm very suicidal." She started to laugh, this little breaking-glass laugh I wish I could imitate. It sounds so amazingly weird. "Yeah, I would say I want to die."

"For real?" I like to imagine being dead, but being *really* dead?

"Look, my little brother had his head out the window because he liked the wind to blow his hair back. The house down the road had one of those monstrous huge mailboxes in the same shape as the house itself? Like a gigantic mailbox in the shape of a fucking TUDOR HOUSE?" I knew what she was going to say, all of a sudden, and I started to creep backward. But I ran into a wall. "It took his head off. Off! Like, one minute Robbie was sitting there and the next minute the whole windshield and the front seat and I were covered with blood and there was nothing anyone could do and I had tried to pull him back in because he was always doing that and how am I supposed to get over that? Ever? Huh? Even if my parents forgive me and my brother Elliott forgives me and my aunts forgive me and my cousins forgive me and the pope forgives me and Jesus forgives me." She stopped. "Would you like to live with that? I'd like to live, but only if they could put a needle in my brain and take out that memory."

"I'm so sorry, Suzette!" I said, and I tried to put my hand on her arm. She jerked away as if I'd tried to throw boiling water on her.

"No one touches me, bitch," she said.

"I'm not a bitch!" I said.

"I know. It's just what I say," Suzette explained, and smiled. She was ultra-creepy sometimes. "Anyhow, are you a cutter?"

"No, I'm not," I said, "but . . ."

"You want to, right?"

"I think so, but not . . . so much. Not *professionally*."

"You can just drag a pen or a razor blade—"

"A razor blade!"

"Yeah, dig one out of your shaver . . . it doesn't really hurt."

"It's got to totally hurt."

"Put ice on it first," Suzette suggested.

So that's what I did. One night after dinner, I put ice on my arm until it was so numb it felt like a doll arm, and then I dug a little wiggly trench along the top of my forearm almost to the elbow, and I let it bleed all over the sheets and the pillowcase. I started to cry. I couldn't believe I was the same little girl who sang her heart out in *Annie* and sat up in the tree in the backyard, hiding from my mom so I didn't have to go to piano lessons. I was here, just four years later, lying on these crummy stiff sheets, doing this. What a comedown. What a disgrace. You can't imagine. And it really did hurt—like my arm was on fire—when the ice wore off. I cried even louder then. Louder and louder, until I was sobbing like a baby. I wasn't some pitiful head case. I was Hope Shay! The things that brought me here didn't seem to link together anymore. I thought I'd understood how it all happened. But now I couldn't be so sure. All I could see was myself, alone, falling down through space into darkness. Logan and Alyssa and Brook and my parents were just faces on the walls rushing by as I fell past them. They were all smiling, as if they were urging me on. *You go, girl!* Or maybe not. Maybe they wanted me to stop before it was too late. The blood was stopping when I looked down. It wasn't a very deep cut. But it was a real mess. I would have passed out from fear if they hadn't found me.

But they did. I forgot about the cameras. This place is, like, all about security. Some guard must have seen what I was doing on his monitor or something. They came for me right away. Suzette was right. They did treat you like a movie star. It was like I was a wounded soldier in battle being wheeled to the infirmary, and then a nurse sat with me for twenty-four hours, feeding me ice cream from a spoon and giving me painkillers.

But on the third day, I ended up sitting with a big wad of gauze wrapped around my arm, in the office of this doctor who looked familiar, though I was sure I never saw her before. She looked like some kind of wildlife biologist on TV, with streaky blond hair and khaki pants.

"Hope," she said, "in all our weekly sessions, you've never talked about having suicidal tendencies."

"I just want someone to believe me. . . ." I began. "Weekly sessions?" Someone was nuts here, her or me. I was afraid to learn which. But I had a feeling I was going to anyway.

SEARCH FOR MISSING STUDENT INTENSIFIES

BY TIMOTHY KEWPRISIN
AND TRACY CLARK

DETROIT, Mich. (AP) — The largest search for a missing person in the history of Michigan's Upper Peninsula ramped up another notch today when volunteer and National Guard pilots began flyovers of the wooded area surrounding Starwood Academy, searching for Hope Shay, the 15-year-old student who disappeared from her dormitory room late last Wednesday night.

An aspiring young actress from the Chicago suburbs, Hope was reported missing by her dorm advisor early Thursday when she failed to show up for breakfast or lunch.

The advisor, Lisa Zurin, 22, told police that the door to Hope's room was open and her purse, as well as a book, was on the bed, which was neatly made. She had apparently been studying. Despite the cold, Hope apparently took no coat or other exterior clothing, just one of the puzzling facts of this disappearance, which may be linked to a threat that the girl described to her mother some weeks ago.

A massive search—including volunteers from Michigan, Wisconsin, and northern Minnesota—resumed today when police failed to find Hope after a 12-hour search of the school grounds, 100 wooded acres outside Black Sparrow Lake. They questioned the girl's friends, teachers, and local residents who might have seen her.

A videotape from a security camera in the lobby of the Lakeside Women's Dormitory at Starwood revealed Hope pacing back and forth in front of the locked glass doors at 1:30 a.m. Thursday morning, as if watching for someone to arrive, according to school officials. The tape, which scans the first floor in segments at 10-minute intervals, showed an empty foyer at 1:40 a.m. In itself, said Zurin, "That wasn't unusual behavior for Hope, because she was often up until all hours. I was always telling her that she needed more sleep."

But police said they doubt that Hope's departure was voluntary, especially after revelations by her mother that a stranger in a truck had harassed Hope on two occasions in recent weeks as she made her way home from rehearsal.

Warren Godchalk, chief of security for Starwood, said he found the statements disturbing because there were no witnesses to the incidents, and Godchalk said students are never allowed to walk on campus unescorted during evening hours. Hope was accompanied to and from rehearsal by a team of seniors designated as escorts.

Hope's parents were in Michigan to see her appear in a performance of *Romeo and Juliet* for local students. She apparently disappeared sometime late Wednesday night or early Thursday morning.

Marian Romano, Hope's mother, saw the threat of an intruder near the school as a very ominous sign.

"Hope thought it was a prank, but she was frightened," she said. Hope's parents are Mark and Marian Romano, of Bellamy, Ill., a suburb of Chicago.

Marian Romano said, "She and the young man in her production were taking extra rehearsal time because she wanted her portrayal to be perfect." Though Romano is the family name, Hope used the name Hope Shay professionally.

The young man has been identified as Logan Rose, already an accomplished actor with film and TV credits, who had decided to finish high school and college before becoming a professional actor, according to his mother.

He said he continued to be involved in the search and wished Hope's family only the best, though he went onstage as Romeo the night after she disappeared.

Hope was understudying the

leading role in Starwood's winter production of *Romeo and Juliet*. Broadway actor Brook Emerson, guest director of the play, announced that he would personally offer a $10,000 reward for information that led to Hope's recovery.

"She is a remarkable young woman," said Emerson, a Tony Award–winning actor and vocalist who starred as Antonio Delleo in *Feast of Fools* in 2004. "Her emotions are very close to the surface, as they are for any actor. But she is also very levelheaded and directed onstage, and there would be no way that she would deliberately leave Starwood on her own."

Black Sparrow Lake Public Safety Director William Flaxen agreed, saying that after interviewing friends, relatives, and instructors, "We have to view this disappearance as a possible abduction."

Police are asking students and residents in and around Starwood Academy to report any suspicious or unfamiliar individuals in the area. Fliers will be posted as far away as Minneapolis and Detroit, where police officials in those cities are cooperating in the search. The fliers show a recent photo of Hope, who is 5'3" tall and weighs no more than 100 pounds.

She was last seen wearing a black Abercrombie & Fitch "hoodie" and matching running pants, with white New Balance tennis shoes.

"Hope was an obsessive runner," said a fellow student, Alyssa Lyn Davore, whom Hope understudied in the play. "She was very small and thin, and she wanted to stay that way. None of us can imagine going on with the play if she's still missing this weekend, but that's what they teach you to do. If I had anything to do with this, I'm heartbroken. I know that Hope was envious of me being Juliet. We all told Hope to lighten up because she was too serious for a kid. Maybe we teased her a little, but it was all in fun."

Security is exceptionally tight because of the isolated rural woodland location, but the alarms did not go off that night, according to Andrea Ross Lobelier, Starwood's women's dean.

Lobelier said, "She may have left. She may have been forced. We can't make that kind of judgment. Hope was an unpredictable young lady. But all teenagers have their moments, especially creative types." She further revealed that Hope had been disciplined once, earlier in the fall, for trying to leave her dorm at night, a strictly forbidden practice, but that she was generally a good student.

"Right now," Lobelier said, "all of our prayers and thoughts are with Hope and her family. We are asking anyone who may have seen her to come forward. There has to be an explanation for this, and we think it will be a natural explanation, and that Hope will be safe."

Starwood Security Chief Godchalk said that search dogs had to be given a day of rest following the full-day effort on Friday and into the early hours of Saturday morning, but that several professional trackers were making their way from as far away as Madison, Wisconsin, with their own canines.

Those with any information regarding Hope are asked to contact the school or the Black Sparrow Lake Department of Public Safety immediately.

An anonymous tip line has been set up at 505-555-1111 for those who may have information about Hope.

Meanwhile, an ever-widening circle of volunteers continue the search throughout the night. Colder temperatures are predicted, raising fears about Hope's safety.

Students at the school held a candlelight vigil, singing "Amazing Grace" outside Hope's window, where her dorm advisor has placed an electric candle that burns night and day.

"We see it as a 'beacon of hope'," Zurin said. "We hope she's out there and knows we care."

HOPE IS ALIVE!

By TRACY CLARK

DETROIT, Mich. (AP) — Hope Shay, 15, who disappeared apparently without a trace last Thursday, was found alive and unharmed today.

Remarkably, the girl suffered only minor abrasions and dehydration, and was found just one mile from her dormitory at Starwood, the exclusive arts academy where she is a student.

William Flaxen, director of the Department of Public Safety in Black Sparrow Lake, said Hope was rushed to St. Mary's Hospital early Monday, after a volunteer rescue tracker, Kavanaugh Hill, and her tracking Saint Bernard, Luther, found the girl in a shallow ditch about a mile from her dorm, not far past an abandoned hunting cabin.

Her condition is described as good.

Armed police officers immediately surrounded the area as Hope was removed in an ambulance, in the belief that her abductor might be apprehended nearby. No one was found in the area, however.

It became apparent early in the search that someone had recently used the cabin, Flaxen said, because there were signs of habitation, such as food wrappings and remnants of a recent fire in the woodstove. Flaxen said he thinks that the individual responsible for Hope's kidnapping probably was using the cabin as a refuge.

Spirits rose when searchers came across a sleeping bag and other items in the hunting cabin early on the second morning of the rescue effort. They at first believed that Hope might have been using it as a hiding place.

But a search of the cabin, while it turned up beer cans and other trash as well as the sleeping bag, yielded no sign of the missing girl.

Flaxen also said that the remains of a roll of duct tape used to bind Hope's hands and feet were found on the piece of ground where she lay, nearly out of sight in a shallow dry ditch under a small bridge about 200 yards from the cabin. Hope had pushed and dragged herself halfway out of the ditch during an epic struggle that included a night when the temperature plummeted to ten degrees F.

"She's a real fighter," said Flaxen.

Hope was treated for minor cuts and exposure, given IV fluids, and released to her parents at approximately 4 p.m. today.

"She's in remarkably great shape for being out there four days," said Flaxen. "It's something of a miracle. She's a very strong young woman."

Through tears, Marian Romano, Hope's mother, who also was treated for exhaustion at St. Mary's, told reporters, "We're so grateful to Miss Hill and to all the students and police and volunteers who helped find our girl, including our friends from Bellamy and the staff and students at Starwood for their hard work and prayers. By the fourth day, even the police were starting to give up. It just seemed like she'd vanished into thin air."

Based on a description and composite sketch, police are seeking a stocky, dark-skinned man of Indian or Latino descent for questioning in connection with the abduction.

Volunteers and police, including detectives from as far away as Minneapolis and Detroit, as well as FBI and Michigan Bureau of Investigation officials, had combined in one of the largest searches ever to have been carried out in the north woods area of Michigan's Upper Peninsula.

The only comparable case

was that of Timmy Underhove, a 6-year-old boy who wandered away from his family's campsite with the family dog in 1999 and was found unharmed three days later, apparently protected by the dog, which the boy said had been attacked by a bear.

Underhove's father and older brother were among those who came to Black Sparrow Lake to search through Friday night for Hope.

Helicopters and light planes, from both local glider clubs and the Michigan National Guard, conducted flyovers of the area Saturday and Sunday, after police and canine units did an exhaustive search, including interviews with all of Hope's classmates and instructors.

Hope was first reported missing by her dorm advisor at the prestigious Starwood Academy of the Performing Arts, Lisa Zurin, when she failed to show up for meals on Thursday.

"At first I thought it was nerves over opening night. But I decided to check, and I'm so glad I did. I can't tell you what a dark cloud hung over this place when she was missing," Zurin said today. "Hope is a new student, and no one knows her very well, but she was one of our own."

Zurin said that Hope had seemed troubled in recent weeks, an observation that was corroborated by Starwood dean of women Andrea Ross Lobelier, who had spoken with Hope on two occasions, once about a disturbing weight loss early in the semester and once about Hope's tendency to leave the dorm late at night—a strict violation of academy rules.

Warren Godchalk, chief of security for the school, said that it was forbidden for young students such as Hope even to go running alone, but that Hope, as well as others, sometimes slipped "through the loopholes" with that rule.

"In her case, it proved to be a dangerous risk," Godchalk said. "It shows that people can be vulnerable even in broad daylight." Hope said she went out to jog at dawn, around 6 a.m.

In retrospect, Lobelier and others said that Hope's apparent mishap may have stemmed from two disturbing encounters she confided in her mother, but did not tell school authorities.

Flaxen said that Hope allegedly was accosted by a man who grabbed her just outside her dorm while she was on an early-morning jog, knocked her unconscious with a "padded" blunt object of some kind, and left her tied in the ditch.

According to Hope, the man spoke of a ransom he hoped to realize from Hope's parents, Mark and Marian Romano of Bellamy, Illinois. No ransom note, however, was ever received.

"The guy apparently got cold feet when we reacted so quickly," Flaxen said. "That meant even a more potentially dangerous situation for the girl, because there were no clues as to her whereabouts at all. She could have been here, or she could have been in California by now."

Despite apparent inconsistencies in the case, which included security-cam footage of Hope apparently either looking for someone or trying to leave her dorm at approximately 1:30 a.m. on Thursday, Flaxen said the case was being considered a kidnapping. He also said that a piece of evidence recovered from the hunting cabin—details of which are being withheld—would be key in finding the individual responsible.

Those who may have seen the driver of an older, dark pickup truck, answering the description given by Hope, are asked to contact the Black Sparrow Lake Department of Public Safety or Warren Godchalk at 505-555-6206.

The same anonymous tip line that was set up for information leading to Hope's recovery, 505-555-1111, is still in operation while police search for leads to finding her captor. An anonymous reward fund for such information, set up at the State Bank of Black

Sparrow Lake, already has accumulated contributions in the amount of more than $2,000.

A service of thanksgiving is scheduled for well-wishers and friends at Six Spruces Chapel in Black Sparrow Lake for 2 p.m. Saturday afternoon. Hope is expected to attend. She is resting from her ordeal but said she was overwhelmed with gratitude at "how much people cared."

"We are a community here," said Dean Lobelier. "When one of us is hurt, all of us are hurt. We couldn't have hoped for a better outcome to this frightening situation."

Police: Hope's Kidnap a Hoax!

By TRACY CLARK

DETROIT, Mich. (AP) — Police in the small town of Black Sparrow Lake, Michigan, have given up the search for a suspect in the kidnapping of Hope Shay, 15, after evidence and an indirect admission from the young student indicated that the girl herself staged her alleged kidnapping.

Kelly Worwitz, spokesman for the Black Sparrow Lake Department of Public Safety, said, "We don't think there ever was a suspect, and we don't think there was a kidnapping."

Black Sparrow Lake Public Safety Director William Flaxen and other investigators determined—after interviews with Hope, her parents, fellow students at the Starwood Academy of the Performing Arts, and merchants at the Lakewood Shopping Nook—

that Hope probably had carefully planned what first appeared to be an abduction by a stalker.

It is furthermore believed that Hope acted alone. Police learned that she purchased long underwear and the duct tape used to bind her hands and feet.

The story of Hope's disappearance spread as far as Australia and England, and a massive outpouring of sympathy, including cards and prayer vigils, poured in from around the world.

She was found unharmed early Monday morning, four days after she had disappeared.

"We don't know what possible motive she could have," said Flaxen in an exclusive interview. "This girl did go through at least one or two terrible nights of exposure. While we have sympathy for her family, we have to be outraged at the amount of money and manpower that was expended searching for her."

Flaxen said that the cost of the four-day search for Hope was in excess of $100,000. FBI and Michigan investigators, National Guard personnel, and volunteer searchers in the hundreds from as far away as Detroit and Chicago joined in the hunt.

The major break in the puzzling case came when a merchant at Lakewood Shopping Nook's Snowy Owl Dry Goods produced a videotape that showed Hope making a purchase including lightweight long underwear, a knife, waterproof duct tape, a waterproof flashlight, and other items that she said were used to subdue and tie her up in the abduction.

The tape and knife were found discarded at the site in the woods where Hope was discovered.

She also purchased power bars, concentrated water packets, and bottled mineral water, the remnants of which were found in a hunting cabin 200 yards from the wooded area.

Flaxen said those items, as well as a mobile phone and

a sleeping bag, originally believed to belong to the kidnapper, now are believed to have been used by Hope as she waited for the right time to bind her own hands and lie down in the gully.

"She couldn't have been comfortable, because that cabin has no heat except a rotted old potbellied stove," Flaxen said. "But she apparently used that and the sleeping bag, as well as some hand-warming packs, to keep warm. She would definitely have suffered frostbite otherwise."

It is not known whether Hope actually spent one night or two nights in the ditch after she tied herself up, convincingly enough that investigators were sure that the kidnapping was genuine.

Hope had told her mother and later told investigators from the Black Sparrow Lake Police and the Federal and Michigan Bureaus of Investigation that a short, dark-haired man of Latino or Indian descent had hit her with a "soft-coated" club of some sort, knocking her unconscious, and that she awoke alone, bound and gagged.

She said that the same man had called to her from an old truck twice on earlier occasions, frightening her because he allegedly knew her name. Police began circulating a composite sketch of her alleged captor created from Hope's description. The drawing also was published in newspapers all around the Midwest.

Based on the sketch, police questioned Alberto Mendez, an assistant manager at Chatters, a café in the Lakewood Shopping Nook. But it turned out that Hope had simply seen Mendez during her weekly shopping trips to the mall with other students.

Mendez says he holds no ill feelings. "Anyone who looks the slightest bit different around here stands out," he said. Mendez's family has lived in Black Sparrow Lake since the early 1900s.

Questions arose after the police interviewed Mendez and Carl Schwartzberg, the owner of Snowy Owl, and reviewed the tapes.

Interviews with Hope also were riddled with inconsistent statements, and her account of the alleged abduction changed constantly, according to Worwitz. The official end of the search was announced in a press release issued just before 9 a.m. today.

It is now apparent that Hope may have been aware that she was the subject of a search the entire time, and in fact was seen jogging during the period when she was supposed to have been tied up in a gully.

One of the first hints that something was amiss with her story was evidence police discovered that someone had logged onto the Internet using Hope's password, checking weather reports and news stories about the "abduction." Hope's cell phone was on her when she was found. It was dusted for fingerprint evidence, but the only finger-

prints found were Hope's. Comparison fingerprints were obtained from items such as her water glass in her dormitory bathroom.

Jim O'Malley, an off-duty forest service officer, also reported encountering a young woman wearing clothes that matched the clothes Hope was described as wearing when she vanished while running near Starwood.

The girl was jogging in the area of the hunting cabin Saturday, O'Malley remembered, because it was one of his days off from his job as a forest service officer. But O'Malley was unable to see her face because she wore a black ski mask.

Hope's parents, Marian and Mark Romano of the Chicago suburb of Bellamy, Illinois, immediately issued a statement through Clark Neeland, a partner in Romano's law firm.

"Hope's parents are shattered, and are pleading with the news media and others to give them the privacy and time to deal with this news as a family. They are deeply sorry for the effort and appreciate each prayer and hope that Hope's actions, however motivated, elicited," Neeland said. "They are grateful to the police, to all the professional and volunteer searchers, and to the school that their daughter was found and is safe. The only thing worse that could have come from this incident would have been for Hope to have suffered grave physical harm."

Police and hospital personnel were initially puzzled at how healthy the 5'3", 100-pound girl was after several nights in the open woodland. On one of those nights, the temperature dipped to ten degrees above zero.

From her statement, it seems that Hope was outside that night and possibly the following night, but spent at least one other night inside the cabin, the police spokesperson said.

The young woman could face charges of fraud that could mean time in a juvenile facility, according to Worwitz. It is not clear yet whether charges will be filed, according to Mesquakie County District Attorney Michael Harlowe's office. A representative of Harlowe's office said "a further investigation into Hope's emotional condition will help determine that."

Worwitz added, "So many people have told us that she was in a very poor mental state just before the incident. We need to determine whether she understood the gravity of her actions."

Hope's parents said she would not be returning to Starwood Academy. According to Neeland, every effort will be made by the family to make sure that Hope receives any medical help that she needs.

Investigators from Michigan traveled to Illinois to continue to interview the Romano family at their home, where they remained in seclusion today, about the aftermath of the largest manhunt in the history of Michigan's Upper Peninsula.

Despite revelations about the fraudulent kidnapping, Godchalk said the predominant mood on the Starwood campus remained one of relief, not revenge.

"Kids here feel sorry for Hope," he said. "They are trying to imagine the loneliness and desperation that would lead a kid to do this." Godchalk added that counselors had been invited to the campus for "debriefing" sessions with the student body, so that they can talk out their feelings about the incident. One student, who asked not to be identified, said that Hope felt "jilted" by an older student, Logan Rose, who appeared as Romeo in the production in which Hope was an understudy, though Rose's family has said the two were only casual friends.

Contacted at his home in Brooklyn and told of Hope's role in the strange occurrence at Starwood, Tony Award–winning actor Brook Emerson—the guest director who chose Hope to understudy the role of Juliet and who contributed most of a $15,000 reward for Hope's recovery—commented only, "I think Shakespeare said it best. 'For never was a story of more woe than this of Juliet and her Romeo.' "

X

'M NOT SUPPOSED TO have these news articles.

But naturally, I looked them up in the library and made copies. I pasted them in a scrapbook, including the pictures. And I studied them. They're proof. They say you can't believe what you read in the newspaper. But without them, I would never have been able to believe what they told me in the office, a few days after I cut my arm.

I mean, later, bits of thoughts started coming to me— sort of like a dream, you know?

I guess getting pushed and pushed like I was when I was a kid, and being loved the way I was (like one day yes, one day no) can let some pretty weird ideas move into your mind.

"X" (See? Remember what I said?) marks the spot where Hope is buried. And it marks the end of this journal.

I started it months and months ago.

And I hardly ever take out the journal and look at it anymore.

I've written other journals over the years, but not like this one. This journal was both the beginning and the end of the most important part of my life so far. "So far" is the key phrase. I know I'm going to have a life afterward now.

I don't need the journal anymore, because I'm a new person now. My name is Bernadette Romano. When I was Hope Shay, a teenage actor, I faked my own kidnapping because I thought it would help me get my boyfriend back. Well, he was never my boyfriend. I thought it would make him notice me and fall for me the way I had fallen for him. It was just a teenage crush that got way, way, way out of control.

Okay?

You have no idea how long it took me to be able to say that and not be faking it when I said it. At first it was just because it made people think I was all fine, and it was what they wanted to hear. But I'd been telling people what they wanted to hear all my life. You see? In order to get their approval? And that was part of the problem, if not the whole root of it. Finally, with a lot of work and thought, I felt able to sort of lift up a corner of the truth. And it looked familiar.

The woman who looked like she was on safari and used to come to our dorm meetings sometimes? I thought she was a teacher, but she was really a psychologist. Anyway, that first day I started therapy with her, it felt like I was hallucinating. She had to *point out* that my parents were there in the room with us. And that was a total shock! I hadn't even noticed them. She said she had deliberately asked them to wait to come to see me until I was out of the infirmary after I cut myself. That's the policy at Taylor Hill. That's what it's called. Taylor Hill. That's where I "go to school." Infirmary visits, she said, tend to make families go all limp and want to take their kids out of this place. Taylor Hill used to be a convent, and then a convent school, hence all the stained glass and leaded glass on the windows.

But not for the past forty years.

It's a different kind of school now.

The first thing the doctor said was, "I want your parents to move across the room and face you, Hope. Is that okay?"

"Is this going to be like Miss Taylor's jam sessions. . . ?" I began. I didn't want any part of that. But my mother and father took each other's hands and went and sat on a sofa across from me. My mother was already crying.

"Her name is Miss Tyler, not Miss Taylor," said the doctor. "And I'm Dr. Lopez. Miss Tyler is a junior counselor.

A junior counselor lives on every ward. She lives on yours, except during her breaks, and then she's replaced by another intern. She isn't there to help you get better, but to help you stay healthy until you get better."

"Then who's Miss Taylor?" I was honestly totally baffled.

"Hope, there is no Miss Taylor. This place is called Taylor Hill because it's built on Taylor Hill."

"But Miss Taylor. I saw Miss Taylor!"

"I think you've been imagining a lot of things, Hope." My parents just sat there. "I don't mean you've been doing that on purpose. I mean that sometimes, when things are just too hard to deal with, one part of us can just see what she needs to see. The other part ignores what she doesn't want to see. What you needed to see was . . . this Miss Taylor."

"A big, heavyset woman? Like Em?"

I saw my parents look at each other, and my mother started to cry even harder.

"You don't really like big, heavy women, do you, Hope?"

"I don't have anything against them," I said.

"But you associate them with things you don't want to be, like fat, right?" asked Dr. Lopez.

"Kind of."

"Well, Miss Tyler is big and very well-muscled, but not

fat. And Em . . . Hope, we really, really need to discuss Em."

"Em? Em is the only good thing about this place."

"Tell me about this place," said Dr. Lopez.

"It's a private boarding school," I began.

"It's a treatment facility," she said. "And we do have an excellent educational component."

"Like a jail?"

"No, Hope. Like a hospital."

"Did it used to be a church?"

"No." Dr. Lopez sat up straighter. "It used to be a convent school. A boarding school run by nuns. Why?"

"Because of the leaded glass."

"Well, there is some ornamental glass. But the windows have . . . well, I hate to call them . . . bars, but they are bars, because we don't want the girls who live here to leave unsupervised or hurt themselves."

"By jumping out? You mean, people like Suzette?"

"Yes, Suzette is . . . we're trying to get Suzette to forgive herself."

"She told me. She never will."

"We think she will. We think Suzette's suicide attempts are more of a cry for help—"

"Oh please," I said. "If someone uses that old phrase again, I'll puke."

"But what did you do with your arm? And what did you do at Starwood?"

"Logan . . ."

"You wanted him to love you the way you loved him."

"He did," I said. "Until Alyssa Lyn."

"I asked Logan to write to you, Hope. A long time ago. So that when you were ready, you could hear his letter. I asked him to write a letter to you and tell you what his feelings were about your pretending to be abducted and the huge effort that went into looking for you. I want to read it to you."

"Is it written to me?"

"Yes."

"Then I don't think you should read it."

"It's written to you, at my request. To help you understand what Logan's real feelings were and are. So I'm going to read it." I just sat there. She opened a single piece of paper. "He writes,

'Dear Hope,

I hope you are feeling better. I know you went through a lot. And I know part of it was my fault. Hope, when I met you, I noticed the same things that everyone notices about you. You were so talented for being as young as you were. And I thought you were very attractive. But you were so much younger than I was that I knew it would be wrong to encourage your having a crush on me.

'So, after tryouts, when you were so sad that you didn't get Juliet, but you were the understudy, I took you out for a cheeseburger. And then, it was like you didn't get that I was just trying to be your pal. You acted like we were together. You would run up and hug me and jump up and wrap your legs around my waist. You would take my sunglasses and put them on. I tried to treat you like a kid sister, but you were calling my phone thirty or forty times a day. You were following me around campus all the time. Every time I had a date with someone, you would write me these hysterical letters about some plan or some idea.

'Hope, there was never any plan. There was never any idea. When they found you, I didn't know what they were talking about. I think you just so badly wanted the kind of attention you used to get back home and you didn't get at Starwood that you flipped out a little. And I don't blame you for trying to put the blame on me. If you really had yourself convinced that we were a couple, and you thought that I was going away on you, I could see how you would feel completely betrayed. And you are a really good kid, and a really talented kid. But you got obsessed with me. And that's what made you do what you did, I think.

'I personally don't believe I was worth all the trouble and pain you put yourself through. I'm just this dumb guy. I really want you to be happy, Hope. Maybe acting is too superficial and stressful for you. Maybe not. But whatever you do, take the time to get better first.

'Your friend, Logan Rose.'

That's what he wrote, Hope. Does that sound right to you?"

It didn't sound right, but it didn't sound wrong, either. It was as though someone I used to be had gotten up and left the room. I didn't know if I liked her, even, but I missed her.

"I . . . I don't know," I said.

"And your friend," said Dr. Lopez.

"Em."

"You don't have a close friend yet, Hope. You paid a lot of attention to a certain girl, but she doesn't even live on your floor. She lives on a floor for girls who are seriously, seriously in trouble. She only comes upstairs for group, because we think it does her good to be around girls who have things to say. From what we can gather through our conversations, your parents and I, you had her confused in your mind with another person. Do you know the person I mean, Hope? Think hard."

"Sort of," I said.

"Do you want your mother to help you remember?" Dr. Lopez asked softly, really gently. I put my hands over my ears.

"I don't know," I said.

"I think it's important. Because we don't want you to feel the way Suzette does, as if you have to punish yourself. Fortunately, what happened to you wasn't as serious as what happened to Suzette. Or to the person you think of as 'Em.' Now, Em is real. You didn't see someone who wasn't there. She struggles with obesity, and her name is Emily Shide, and she was a dancer at one point, a very promising dancer. And it is true that you talk to Emily Shide whenever you see her, at meals and in group and after group. And while she doesn't ever talk, she does respond in some way to you. Which is a good thing."

"And so?"

"Well, there's one thing about Emily that you seem to think is true, from the notes you wrote and signed with her name."

"That *I wrote*? She wrote notes to me all the time."

"Hope, Emily hasn't communicated by writing or speaking for more than two years. She understands, but she doesn't communicate. You wrote both sides of the correspondence, if you will, which is not a totally atypical thing for a girl with what would be called a borderline personality—if you were older; you're too young for me to make that kind of diagnosis."

"What do you mean, borderline?"

"Well, in simple terms, it means being on the borderline

between sane and not so sane. You were on the other side of the border for a while. And now we think you can move from that dangerous side to the side that's good for you. We want to help you do that. Do you know why you got so attached to Emily, and why you always call her 'Em'? She never called herself that, according to her parents."

"Mom?" I said, in that little, squeaky, Alice-in-Wonderland voice.

"Hope, darling."

"Call her Bernadette right now," said Dr. Lopez. "I think it's time for that."

"Bernadette, my sister Marjorie was a dancer," said my mother.

"Stop!" I told her. She started to cry really hard.

"Go ahead, Marian," said Dr. Lopez.

"My sister Marjorie was a dancer. And when she was seventeen, she was in the corps de ballet at the Joffrey, in New York, where we lived when you were born. You know that we lived in New York when you were born," she said, and I nodded. "Well, Marjorie was six years younger than I was, just as my sister Margaret is six years older. I was already married and you were a little child when she . . . when she . . ." My mother looked at my father for help.

"Go on, Marian," Dr. Lopez said.

"When she was almost eighteen, she got . . . she got pregnant with one of the boys who was in the touring company. And our mother, Grandma Shay, well, our mother was very ambitious for Marjorie. So, she basically forced Marjorie to have an abortion. But it . . . didn't work. It ended the pregnancy, but it also hurt Marjorie. There was a mistake made by the doctor. Marjorie had to have another operation, and it meant she couldn't ever have any children." My mother looked at Dr. Lopez, who kind of bit her lips together and nodded.

"I can't," my mother said.

"She needs to know how this started," said Dr. Lopez.

"Well, after that Marjorie shut herself up in her room. She was healthy enough to dance again, but she wouldn't do it. She wouldn't even come out. All she ever did was to come out long enough to go to the store and buy . . . candy. She gorged herself on candy until she weighed more than two hundred and fifty pounds. And she wouldn't wash her hair or get out of bed—"

"That's just like Em!" I said. "Mom, that's totally—"

"That's what we called her," said my mother. "We called ourselves Three-M. That was the name of an old company that made sticky tape. Three-M. Our parents called us that, too, when we were kids. But as we grew up, she was the only one we still called M as a nick-name, because she didn't like her first name. She thought it was too old-fashioned."

"But I didn't know that!"

"You did," my father said. "You always had a killer memory, Detta. And you remembered, or we think that you remembered, things that your mother and I said about her sister. We know you remembered her, because you would point to the picture of her in her dance costume that Mom has in her room. You would actually say, 'Em.' Marjorie's death was one reason I didn't want you pushed into acting so hard, despite how talented you are—"

"She died?" I gasped.

"Yes, Hope," my mother said, crying so hard that snot was running out of her nose and she was choking. "Yes, she died at a place not much different from this one. Very like Taylor Hill. My parents brought her there to get better. But she committed suicide."

"She cut her wrists," I said.

"I thought you were too little to understand, when we would refer to her," my mother said. "You were no more than three or four when she died. We talked about her a lot then. Afterward, we moved. And we hardly mentioned her when you were older. But you always had this phenomenal memory. You could repeat whole nursery rhymes when you were eighteen months old, before other children could even say their own names!" My mother was crying hard, now, harder than I'd ever seen her cry. Except once. A long time ago. It was as though I was seeing her through a gauze curtain, much younger, in a back dress, in a big church. . . .

"Did I know your sister?"

"Yes, she was your favorite person," my father said gently. "Before she shut herself away, she would sing and dance for you. You would clap your hands. She loved you so much. And part of the reason that your mom's other sister, Aunt Margaret, barely speaks to your grandmother Shay is because she thinks Grandma Shay was responsible for Marjorie's death. Aunt Margaret acted and sang onstage too, when she was very young, just as your mother did. But she stopped when Marjorie died."

"And so . . ." my mother said, sitting up straighter.

"Marian, tell her the rest," said Dr. Lopez.

"Well, when you came here, and you were convinced that there was a girl named Em living right down the hall from you, I mentioned my sister. And we put things together."

"Your memories of your aunt were very sweet and tender," said Dr. Lopez. "So naturally, you wanted to tell Emily your story. You were very drawn to her because in some way she reminded you of her aunt. Emily is a very dear girl, in her way."

"Did I ever see Aunt Marjorie when she was fat?"

"Yes," my mother said. "My parents brought her to see us for a few days before they took her to the hospital. She hardly ever spoke to anyone by then, like this girl Emily. But, Hope, I mean, Bernadette, she spoke to you. I believe she thought in some way that you were her little girl."

My father took over then. "And when you told Dr. Lopez about Suzette showing you the scars on her wrists, and then you cut yourself, I knew we had to find some way to tell you because we were so frightened for you. Marjorie tried to kill herself a number of times before she finally did, Detta. They took everything away from her. She finally used a . . . a fountain pen."

"Don't worry," said Dr. Lopez. "The administrators of Taylor Hill have security cameras in every room. Nothing can ever happen again the way it did with Marjorie. We're lucky we have the technology now, so that we can have eyes and ears everywhere. When Suzette does what she does . . . which is never lethal, Bernadette, and I want you to know that, she goes outside to one corner of the exercise pavilion where she knows the cameras don't reach. That's being corrected." I nodded, and she went on, "But Suzette has probably told you that this isn't the first time she's been here, Bernadette. Suzette is twenty-four years old. Her brother died when she was sixteen. It was one of the first times she'd ever driven with him in the car."

"But she looks like me! She looks like she's a kid!"

"Time flows differently for some people," Dr. Lopez said. "Even in the way they think of themselves."

I knew what she meant. I didn't even think of time as real since I'd come to Taylor Hill: Days and nights just seemed to blur one into the other.

"What month is it?" I asked.

"It's May, Bernadette," said Dr. Lopez. I looked outside, and she was right! The flowering crabapple trees were blooming, and there was a robin nest with a mother and three little baby robins right next to her window.

I said, "I thought it was still winter!"

"Well, it's been winter in the place you were living, Bernadette. But now you know it's spring. Do you also know you were never Logan Rose's lover?"

"I loved him," I said.

"I believe that," said Dr. Lopez. "I believe all feelings are real. But you weren't lovers. You've never had sex, Bernadette." And the moment she said that, I realized that was true. I had no memory of sex, just the feeling of how wonderful it would be to be in someone's arms and be that close to someone.

"Bernadette," I said softly. "My name is Bernadette."

"It's a beautiful name," said Dr. Lopez.

"It is," said my father.

I said, "There is no Hope."

"Do you mean the name?" Dr. Lopez asked.

"Yes," I said. "I don't mean the feeling." My shoulders dropped down, and I leaned back against the chair. For some reason I felt relaxed, as though I'd passed through the dark place. "Marjorie liked *Alice in Wonderland*, didn't she?"

"It was her first principal role," my mother said. "She was only twelve. She loved the book, too, and she read it to you. You were too small to understand, but she acted out all the parts, getting bigger and smaller and meeting the white rabbit. We still have her copy. In your memory box."

"Funny," I said.

"What?" Dr. Lopez asked.

"Nothing. Just funny," I said. Some things you get to keep to yourself. Thank heavens there are no security cameras in your mind.

It took me a while to admit it, but Dr. Lopez turned out to be a pretty good person. Still, the way she explained a borderline personality, when she really got into it, sounded pretty much to me like anyone else. How I feel and act toward other people, she told me, is up to me. I don't really need to believe psycho bull. I just have to walk the walk. I'm going to do that.

Dr. Lopez said one clue to how I am is that I don't care enough about other people's feelings. I lack compassion. She asked me why I would ask my grandmother to make mittens for Logan when she had arthritis. Well, I told her, I didn't know how to knit!

"But you're not the center of the universe, Bernadette," she said. "The usual thing would be for you to think of her possible discomfort first, and your need for the mittens second." That exasperated me for a long time. It was like for a psychologist, she had trouble connecting the dots. She asked me dumb question after dumb question. She asked me why I don't plan Christmas presents for my family. I still don't get that. I don't have a job. I don't have any money. Like, what does she expect me to do? Make cards with crayons that say "I Love Mommy"? I'm seventeen now, after all. But after she brought it up, I took money out of my bank account, with my father's permission, and I sent all three of them gift certificates to Techno World last Christmas, so they could buy themselves CDs or movies. And they came here to spend the weekend with me, and brought me a computer, with all this software like games and encyclopedias because we can't use the Internet in here—and new running shoes and a bunch of books and a down comforter. I liked all the stuff, but Dr. Lopez said that a girl with "more feelings" would show how grateful she was for all the things they gave me. She says I need to go out of my way to give more than I take.

I didn't "take" anything, so far as I could see. If someone gives you a down comforter, are you supposed to get all choked up? Are you supposed to give it back? My running shoes were totally worn out.

These "extra feelings" she talks about I didn't get. And I still don't entirely. I didn't know how people get "more feelings." Dr. Lopez said, "Take your brother, Carter. The problem with his knee. That's a good case of what I mean."

Carter was this big soccer star, but then he ripped out his knee last year and that was the end.

My mother called and said he was totally devastated. And I said it was lousy, really too bad. But that wasn't enough.

Dr. Lopez got me to make a project of caring about Carter's disappointment, even though it was *Carter* who wasn't getting an athletic scholarship to Boston University, not me. She said if I was brought up to know that I wasn't completely the center of the universe—I found her repeating that over and over kind of insulting at first—I would very naturally "empathize" with my own brother's disappointment. After all, I've had losses in my life, too. Big-time. More than a knee surgery.

So, my assignment was to write to Carter and call

him. And, the thing was, he really appreciated it.

He wrote me a letter that I did find sad. He said this was the most attention I'd ever paid to him and that it was really nice of me. He's going to major in business or law now. He's going to be a sports agent, he says. I call him on the phone now. I make a point of it once a month. I have to tell you, it's okay. Carter's actually a pretty nice person. He's funny, and he has a weird outlook on life, which I like.

I never even knew him.

All those years.

It's not like I'm all crazy about him. But I'm getting to know him, and I have to admit he's more like me than anyone else is, since we have the same parents. Which is a good thing. Dr. Lopez was right that caring gets people to do nice things for you. People like you more for caring than they like you if they just admire you. I think I need that right now. Plus if you have a brother or sister, you can compare notes on how strange your parents are. And my parents are definitely strange, especially now that they have to straight-up cope with a daughter who's a certifiable nutso.

My parents were pretty heavily into what *might* be, instead of what really was. It's tempting to let them pretend I'm at a prep school. But I have to keep a tight hold on fantasies and make sure that they don't get mixed up in my mind with reality.

I probably did do that. I don't do that now.

The reality is, even though I'm a *patient* at Taylor Hill, I'm also a senior now, and a student who got a 1450 on her SATs. I got accepted by the University of Michigan and by Northwestern. I was pretty stupid when I was an actor. But since I had nothing else to do at Taylor Hill, I started hitting the books. And this memory of mine turned out to be very, very useful. I realized that it could be put to other uses than learning song lyrics and monologues.

The SAT score is not a "grandiose fantasy," by the way. Not like thinking I was chosen to play Juliet.

I still have crying jags when the Tony Awards or the Academy Awards are on. But I know I can't go there in my mind. I really shouldn't watch them. It's like an alcoholic going to bartending school.

According to Dr. Lopez, I still have a ways to go, and I'll always be a little like I was. People like me don't "get better." They don't have pills for me. But I can "recognize" how I am. I can understand why, like, my parents didn't do me any favors paying too much attention to me for having talent. It taught me to respond to people in ways that weren't normal. I get that now. Dr. Lopez taught me that too much attention is just as bad for a child as too little.

And she totally nixed even the idea of me going to college in Michigan. Dr. Lopez said that going someplace where I might be tempted to relive that wasn't healthy.

If I go, on deferred acceptance in a year, she said I need to go to Northwestern.

The University of Michigan is too close to where the abduction happened. Okay, fine! I'm not supposed to describe it that way, even to myself. It didn't "happen." I did it! I'll always be the girl who did that. Fine. It pisses me off that this has to be the first thing anyone ever knows about me. I'll, like, probably never be famous for anything the way I was for disappearing myself. That was *two years* ago. But okay! That's how it has to be, or I'm going to be living in a room with bars on the windows for the rest of my life, which I don't plan to do, please.

The very reasons I *wanted* to go to college in Michigan would make it "toxic" for me, according to Lopez.

When she said that, I wouldn't speak to her for a week. I just sat and stared at her in my sessions, and she sat and stared back. She's a pretty tough nut. But so am I. I knew what she wanted me to say. Then, okay, finally, I did. I said, "It's too close to where I faked my abduction. I wouldn't be safe mentally." And at last, she gave me that big, pretty smile and a pat on the arm.

She said, "Good job, kiddo." I might be like a dog performing for liver snacks, but her smiles meant a lot to me then. And they still do. They keep me going. They keep me from slipping back. They reassure me that there's a future out there for me, that I have brains and other talents.

He's on TV now, by the way. Logan Rose. In the show *Guilty Conscience*, the one about this guy who's a medium who can tell if someone has committed a crime, just by being in the same room as that person. I watched it once. I was specifically not supposed to, but how could I not do it? The writing is godawful, and there's always one scene where Logan has to come out in a wife-beater, even though there's absolutely no plot reason at all for him not to have a shirt on. I'll bet he makes a crapload of money; and I know girls, even girls here, who have posters of him in this idiot cowboy hat and boots he wears because the show takes place in New Mexico. He supposedly got, like, his powers because of something that came down from the sky, a little shiny pebble or something he picked up when he was a baby. You know, like Roswell, the alien crash place, in New Mexico.

So subtle.

I'm not supposed to think of things in terms of "plot."

I'm supposed to think in terms of stories that are factual, because what I want to be now is a reporter.

I think.

I mean, it seems interesting enough.

That's how I rationalize that I still have my clippings.

I know it's not the real reason. But I lay the plastic envelopes with the clippings from all the newspapers and the *People* magazine, which had pictures of me in the roles I played when I was a child, under shelf paper in my drawer. I've been moved to a dorm where they don't need security cameras, because I'm not a risk to myself. So I can have a little privacy. And I don't think it's going to put me over the edge to have my clippings. Do you?

Plus, I wasn't really ever a risk to myself.

Not like Suzette. She got out last year, but she's back now for a return engagement. She's got so many cuts she looks like you could pull on her arm and her skin would open, like a window blind. I am glad that I'm not Suzette. She used to fascinate me a little, like a ghost or a witch would entice and scare you all at once, you know? But now, I just feel . . . I feel sorry for her! I feel sorry for Suzette.

Anyway, why I think I might want to be a reporter is that now when I look at those stories, I don't just think about me, but about how the people who wrote them got to ask everyone about all their secrets, to see things that regular people don't get to see. If I become a reporter, I'll be in on things. I'll get to go to crime scenes, which I find semi-interesting. It's a kind of power, you know? I need to feel some power. I have lived "in a place" (as Dr. Lopez would say, and she doesn't mean a city or a town) where somebody else got to say what I ate, where I slept, what I did, even what I said. And I'd like to live in a place where I make the decisions. I know reporters have bosses who tell them what to write about, but they don't tell them exactly how to write it, the exact words to use.

That was the lousy part of being an actor. I never got a chance to be anyone but someone else. I never got a chance to say words that were my own.

The good part was, oh God, the good part was the applause. The total focus on me. The adoration. Being noticed in a way no ordinary person ever is. How do you live without that, I asked Dr. Lopez just last week? How do you live without that if you've had it? What can ever take its place?

She sat there for a long time. Then she got up and came over and put her arms around me, and she's not the huggy type. She sighed, and it was the one time that she was like a mother-type person, even though she's not really old enough to be my mother. She hugged me tight.

She said, "The applause had to come from inside you. That's how it is for most of us, for ninety-nine percent of the world. Someday, Bernadette, no one will have to tell you when you've done something well, because you'll hear the applause inside."